CHARLIE JONES

CHARLIE JONES

A Novel by Ben Harrison

CHARLIE JONES. Copyright © 2025 by Ben Harrison.

All Rights Reserved. No part of this book may be reproduced in any manner including electronic information storage and retrieval systems without permission in writing from the publisher except for pertinent, brief quotations embodied in a critical article or review.

This is a work of fiction. Names, characters, events and incidents are the products of the author's imagination.

3rd Edition
ISBN: 978-1-7364604-6-7
Harrison Gallery & Music Publishing
Key West, FL 33040

Visit the author's website at
www.benharrisonkeywest.com

Cover Design:
Guy Hermelin & Nina Pilar
C. T. & CO., CHICAGO

Printed in the United States of America

Dedicated to my wife of over 50 years, Helen, and our two sons, Benjamin and Cole. It is also dedicated to our children's wives, Lauren and Stephanie Lynn, and our grandchildren—Benny, Roman and Kai.

Table of Contents

Chapter I	There is Good and There is Evil	1
Chapter II	Love and War—Charlie's Parents	19
Chapter III	Jones' Lumber and Hardware	31
Chapter IV	Perpetual Motion	43
Chapter V	Hal, Red, and Oil Wells	51
Chapter VI	Business and Pleasure	67
Chapter VII	Getting to Know You	85
Chapter VIII	The Big Time	95
Chapter IX	The Show	105
Chapter X	A House on the Hill	115
Chapter XI	You Did What?	123
Chapter XII	Robstown	133
Chapter XIII	Par for the Course	139
Chapter XIV	Back with a Plan	149
Chapter XV	Across a Crowded Room	157
Chapter XVI	Hurricane Greta	175

Chapter XVII	Rain, Rain, Rain	183
Chapter XVIII	Life Goes On	195
Chapter XIX	Muscle & Blood; Skin & Bone	209
Chapter XX		221
Chapter XXI	Get Away	233
Chapter XXII	Implementing the Plan	247
Chapter XXIII	Rhythm and Dues	261
Chapter XXIV	The *Harlequin* Gets Wet	275
Chapter XXV	Port Isabel	283

CHARLIE JONES

a novel by Ben Harrison

Chapter I

There is Good *and* There is Evil

THE glistening new white 1959 two-door *Coupe de Ville* Cadillac with spaceship fins turned left off Ocean Drive into the parking lot of the red-brick First Methodist Church of Corpus Christi, Texas.

Before getting out of the driver's side, Mr. Duncan pushed the electric buttons lowering the front two chrome-framed windows so the car wouldn't be "hot as Hades" when the church service was over. Ritualistically, he went around the front of the car to open Mrs. Duncan's passenger-side door. Susan, their 17-year-old daughter, helped push the front seat forward and got out afterwards before he closed the door behind her. Picture perfect, they walked to the shaded patio where donuts were laid out on a folding table with a paper tablecloth. Coffee in hand, the faithful were smoking cigarettes and talking prior to the church bell.

Leaving Mom and Dad in the breeze port, Susan, wearing a white Sunday dress over a petticoat, climbed the stairs to the wing where the young adult Bible classes were held. As Susan walked down the green-polished linoleum hallway in her patent-leather pumps, she thought she saw Charlie Jones standing in the hall next to Mike Ross, a high school classmate who, like Susan, was a member of the Methodist Youth Fellowship. She had no idea why Charlie was there. He looked pale. Something looked wrong.

"Charlie, what are you ... Charlie, what is the matter with you? Are you okay?"

"I think I've got the flu," Charlie murmured, and Susan started smiling even though she wasn't quite sure why. Charlie looked as though he might have the flu, but he smelled like stale tequila and cheap perfume.

"Look," she said feeling motherly and realizing this was a crisis situation, "I don't know what you've been up to, but you smell awful. You can't go into the classroom like that, you just can't. Have you been to sleep?"

This is so unlike Charlie, she thought as she

stepped closer and put her hand on his arm. They'd been friends for a long time.

Charlie wanted to hug her, kiss her and never go to a whorehouse again as long as he lived.

"It seems to be coming from your ears. The perfume, Charlie, how'd you get that awful perfume in your ears? Go wash your face in the bathroom. Start chewing this gum. Hurry, I'll wait for you."

Trying to be inconspicuous, Charlie started seeing black and white spots as he leaned over the basin to wash his face and ears with liquid soap from the wall-mounted dispenser. Nauseous, he unwrapped and put two sticks of Wrigley's Spearmint Gum in his mouth.

"Better," she said when he returned. Susan reached up and put a dab of the perfume she had taken from her small, patent-leather purse with gold clasp and chain. "Maybe you'll pass if you sit next to me. Come on, quickly, we don't want to walk in late."

In the Sunday school classroom with polished floors, white walls and bright florescent lights, Charlie, Mike, Susan and 37 bright-eyed youngsters in their Sunday suits and dresses sat on varnished oak chairs facing the lectern. Susan absent mindedly shook her head and suppressed a smiled as she tried to imagine what the boys had been up to.

Charlie, who felt like throwing up, was trying to pay attention to the plight of Moses, the burning bush and how the Ten Commandments apply to teenagers. At the same time, he was silently asking Jesus to forgive him, a lowly whoremonger, for his unpardonable sins. Overcome with guilt, fear and a monumental hangover, he knew God was disapprovingly looking down on him from above.

"Please, dear God, I promise I will never go to a place like that again. I have sinned. I'll never, ever do it again. Please, dear God."

Susan elbowed him every time he started to close his eyes.

Temptation—the thought of actually doing "it" with a girl—and peer pressure were the forces that drove Charlie Jones, straight "A" student and varsity athlete, down the 150-mile road to "Boy's Town" in Nuevo Laredo, México.

That Charlie would find himself in church the morning after was prophetic. Charlie had never been a church goer because churches, in general, drove both his mother, Evett, and father, "Ivory" up the wall. Ivory thought religion was bullshit and didn't mind saying so, which was heresy in Texas where everyone attended the church of their choice. "Under God" had just been added to the Pledge of Allegiance.

Charlie found himself there after spending the night with Mike Ross whose parents always went to bed early and never waited up for their son. The unwritten rule being, he and any friends staying over, had to go to church the next morning.

Mike told his parents, "Oh, we're going to the movie and get a hamburger at Tri-Drive. Then we're supposed to meet some girls and listen to records." When the horn honked, they headed out the door and piled into a red and white, two-tone Plymouth DeSoto Firedome V-8 with four other boys.

Crossing the border at nine o'clock, they immediately went to the Cadillac Bar where the bartender smiled knowingly as he gave them directions. After a quick beer, they chipped in for a bottle of Sauza Tequila and off they went.

Just as they had been told, there was a policeman in a rumpled tan uniform at the gate who, for 10 pesos, showed them where to park and promised the car would be guarded.

Inside the walled compound was a circular path with bars and toothless whores barking obscene offers at them as they hurriedly walked, wide-eyed, past open doorways. "You want good pussy? I show you. Come. Blow job five dollar."

Trying to look like they knew what they were doing, they went directly to "La Luz Roja," "The Red Light." Inside was a dark room that was almost empty except for girls sitting around looking bored.

Most of the whores hated high school kids, especially if it was hunting season when all the middle-aged men came to hunt dove and fuck. They knew they wouldn't be getting any $20 tips, but the young ones were fast—in and out of there. With a tequila buzz, the boys were coaxed into buying whiskey sours as the girls made their passes and sat on their laps. It was a tough choice because, by that time, they all looked good enough for what they wanted.

Charlie felt a little weird bargaining with her, but that's what he'd been told to do. After the price of $15, down from $20, was agreed upon, bleached-blond "Isabel" with the big tits took Charlie's hand and led him up the stairs to her un-air-conditioned room with a crucifix above the bed. Isabel must have known it was his first time because he kissed her, and everyone knows you don't kiss whores.

With casual indifference she made him unzip her dress and unfasten her bra before she took off her high heel shoes. She was soft around the middle with large dark nipples on breasts that hung lower than he expected.

Charlie's boner didn't care as she unbuttoned his shirt, undid his pants and led him to the bed holding his dick.

"Qué Grande!" Isabel said, "Es big!" That's what she always said.

Knowing he wouldn't last long, she let him fumble around with her chest for a few moments before gently leading him inside a warmth he had never experienced—teeth clenched, eyes closed, holding on tight, what felt like a volcano erupting inside him was rising fast, too fast—impossible to hold back....

Overwhelmed, trying to think, the horny young man with a tequila grin bought her one more time as they showered. After drying off with small rough towels, Isabel put her brassiere back on and stepped into her dress that she had hung on a hook.

"You good." That's what she always said.

"Muchas gracias," he kept saying as she pulled him toward the door and down the stairs. She would need at least three more men if she was going to make money that night, but it was still relatively early. The late-night crowd wouldn't start showing up for an hour or two.

Full of themselves, the boys climbed back into their steel pony and roared back to Corpus Christi, drinking tequila and crowing like roosters.

The stream of sunlight that leaked through the curtains into Charlie's eyes hurt. At first not knowing where he was, Charlie just lay there holding his head. The painful trance he was in was interrupted when Mike's parents knocked on the door. "We're going to the early service, see you boys at Sunday school," they cheerfully called out.

Now, here he was sitting on a hard-oak chair looking at Susan's dress with the bunched-up petticoat touching his leg. Out of the corner of his eye, he could see her hands holding her purse. Boy, they were pretty. Her healthy, smooth, tan legs were crossed at the ankle ... her breast was only inches away from his shoulder.

Jesus, God, he was getting a hard-on in Sunday school.

"I didn't mean you, 'God and Jesus,'" he silently told the deity, but, "Jesus" it kept getting harder as he held it down with his forearm. No one gets a hard-on in church. "Fuck," he said to himself, "Jesus or God, one of them is going to kill me for sure."

Trying to think pure thoughts, it still would not go away. Throbbing, he knew it was going to pop up once he took his arm off it. Sure enough, as Susan got up from her chair, she couldn't help but glance at the obvious upward activity in his slacks. Stifling a laugh, her parting words were, "I hope you get over the flu Charlie Jones, 'cause I think you've been a *bad, bad* boy." Their eyes locked for an instant.

Sitting quietly in the back seat of the big, *Coupe de Ville* on their way to the Club for lunch, Susan wondered who he had been with and how far they had gone. *Jealousy?* Whatever it was, this was exciting because they had been friends for as long as she could remember. When they were in the sixth grade, he had been her first boyfriend. They had slow danced and held hands in a movie. Unsure if it was a kiss, their lips had touched.

At the Corpus Christi Country Club, buffet tables loaded with food were in the center of the ballroom next to the dining area. This Sunday, the slowly melting, glistening ice sculpture set in the middle of an elaborate flower arrangement was a bucking bronco. Susan always put red radishes on her salad plate and almost always got the shrimp curry over rice with chutney on the side—bacon bits and chopped hard boiled eggs on top.

"Are you all right, Susan? Cat got your tongue?" her mother asked as they moved down the long table, her pantyhose making a quiet chafing sound as she walked.

"Fine, Mother. Guess who was in church this morning? Charlie Jones. I couldn't believe it."

Mrs. Duncan liked Charlie and was aware that he and her daughter spoke often on the telephone. Not that she would want her daughter to marry someone like Charlie whose mother was a Mexican, but she liked him a lot more than Gene, the boy Susan had gone steady with for more than a year. Charlie was always polite, well-dressed and well-spoken the few times they had conversed.

Back in the sixth grade, Susan had been a tall, thin gangly girl. Like others her age in 1955, she wore bobby socks with brown and white saddle oxford shoes. Her dresses, hemmed below the knees, were made of soft, patterned cotton, often bright yellow to accentuate her blondish hair. She had red-plaid harlequin style glasses, and held her books over a developing chest. In short, Susan was fashionable by Corpus Christi standards.

She and Charlie had been classmates since the first grade, so Charlie was surprised and caught off guard by what happened to him one afternoon while working with Susan on a science project. Science had become super important in the 1950's because Russia's "Sputnik" was the only satellite circling the earth.

Incidentally, Susan's arm had touched his, and something powerful hit him inside his chest. He couldn't stop thinking about her. It was non-stop. At home, lying in bed, he found himself making up stories where he was the hero, and Susan was faithfully by his side, helping him overcome whatever treachery his imagination conjured up that evening. A revolving theme was being shipwrecked together naked, the wind having blown their clothing to shreds.

Love is a treacherous emotion, especially first love. What if he openly revealed his feelings for her, and she laughed? What if she was in love with someone else? What if his folly got around school? He'd be dead, finished forever, Fool Number One.

At the Six-Points Pharmacy, Charlie, heart racing, began searching for the perfect Valentine's Day card.

Not only did he give her a flowery Valentine, she gave him one that left no doubt she felt the same way. Singing slightly off-key, he was high as a kite riding home on his Schwinn bicycle with wide-handle bars.

> I've got the world on a string,
> Sitting on a rainbow
> Got that string around my finger
> Oh, what a life
> I'm in love.

In Corpus, couples in love attending Robert T. Wilson Elementary School showed their affections in ritualistic ways strange enough to have been beamed down from "Sputnik." First, Charlie had his mom take him to a sporting goods store where he bought a white, nylon football cleat. From sporting goods, they went to Jones' Lumber and Hardware, his dad's store, where he found an eye bolt that would fit the threaded hole of the cleat.

After school the next day, Charlie tagged along behind the group of whispering girls Susan regularly walked home with. When she broke away from her friends and went to her front door, she waited for him as he walked up the sidewalk and put it into her soft, beautiful, wonderful hand.

The next day Susan, wearing the cleat around her neck on a string, gave him a bright multi-colored scarf, which he wore tied around his neck with the knot off to the side. Even though they wore these symbols of love for each other in public, the only time they could really talk was on the phone. The phone was their only time alone together, and they tied up the line for hours. The first time Charlie told Susan he loved her was over the phone ... in Morse code, which he had been learning in Boy Scouts.

When Susan went to camp that summer, Charlie, pockets filled with quarters, clandestinely called her long-distance every Sunday from the pay phone at Lamar Park Pharmacy. Though they told each other, "I love you," when she returned, the spark was missing. By the time they were halfway through the fall semester of junior high, it became clear that their mutual elementary infatuation had died down.

Even so, they remained confidants exchanging secrets about all kinds of things, including juicy gossip that they kept to themselves. That's how she learned to trust him.

Charlie's star shone brightly at Hamlin. He was the starting right guard on the seventh, eighth and ninth grade football teams. Corpus Christi wasn't a mean-spirited place. Most of the kids either didn't know of his Hispanic lineage or think much of it one way or the other. His last name was "Jones".

The movie extravaganza, *Giant*, starring Rock Hudson and Elizabeth Taylor, spoke truthfully and forcefully about prejudice against "Meskins." Rock got the crap beaten out of him while the "Yellow Rose of Texas" blared from Sarge's jukebox as he fought to have a Latino family served in an all-white diner.

> Oh, the Yellow Rose of Texas
> That I am going to see
> Nobody else could miss her
> Not half as much as me
>
> She's the cutest little rosebud
> That Texas ever knew

Her eyes are bright as diamonds
They sparkle like the dew

She cried so when I left her
It like to broke my heart
And if I ever find her
We never more will part

In addition to sports, Charlie served on the student council and was voted "best-all-around male" by his peers his senior year of junior high. He did equally well in high school. Like his parents, there was a light side and a dark side to Charlie. His spontaneous sense of humor made people who met him like him instantly. The dark side wasn't sinister, it was serious. Charlie, even as a young man, took life seriously.

After the Young Adult Sunday School torture, Mike and he managed to avoid their parents until Mike dropped him off at home late in the afternoon. Alone in his bedroom watching a cowboy movie on the black and white portable television that resembled a suitcase, Charlie deeply questioned his morality. Again, he wondered why his father had this thing about churches. He wondered if God wasn't doubly upset with him for screwing a Mexican whore—twice, no less—when his mother was a "Mexican."

Then he thought about Susan, her perfume, her eyes, her chest and her thigh that had been so close to him that morning. His skin still felt warm where she had put her hand on his arm, and he couldn't help but think about what it would be like to do the same things with her that he had done with Isabel.

Biology grabbed him again ... the urge was strong ... her perfume lingered. Leaving the cowboys on the screen, he went into the bathroom, locked the door and tried to keep from rattling the porcelain lid covering the commode reservoir.

On the down side of jerking-off, he went back to his room even more guilt ridden. God was surely going to turn his dick into a bush that was burning yet would not consume itself.

What would he say when he saw Susan at school the next day? Surely, by now, she had some idea how bad he had been. He was sure she had seen what was going on in his pants at church. What would happen to their friendship now that she knew how truly terrible he was on the inside? Would she ever confide in him again?

The next morning, catching up to him after English class, Susan put her hand on Charlie's bicep. With a mischievous twinkle in her eye, she said, "Call me," and doubled back toward her class.

He did, and as soon as she closed the door to her bedroom, "Charlie, did you go to a whorehouse?

"You know what I'm talking about. Charlie. The rumor around school is that you and your football buddies went to Mexico and 'did it.' Is that how the perfume got in your ears?"

Susan couldn't see Charlie involuntarily grinning like a Cheshire cat caught with its paw in the cookie jar, nor would she leave the subject alone. "What was it like, Charlie? What did she look like? Did you like it? Was it your first time? Did you take all your clothes off? Wow! Charlie, I've got to talk to someone about this. You're my friend. You're the only person I can really talk to."

It was provocative, hinting around about what he had or hadn't done. "Did you leave the light on? You took a shower with her!"

He couldn't believe someone as pure as Susan was even curious about something as dirty as sex.

Several telephone conversations later in a barely audible, resigned voice Susan Duncan told him, "I've done it, too." She needed to talk to someone, tell someone, and her confession showed how strong her faith in Charlie was.

At school they were normal towards each other, yet on the phone, they talked intimately about God and hell and sex. That night, she confided that she and Gene, her boyfriend of over a year, had gone all the way, and they had promised each other never to do it again. Gene, a devout Catholic, got really uptight and told her how wrong and how sorry he was. They had both been nervous wrecks hoping she wasn't pregnant.

"I didn't let him do anything for a long time after we started going together, but then one night after a couple of beers I let him feel me up. After a while, I started letting him touch me underneath my blouse, and he would press himself against me.

"Then one night he was on top, making out in the back seat at the drive-in movie. In the heat, he reached down and unzipped his pants. All of a sudden it was there. I froze. It happened so fast. Afterwards I was crying. There was guilt, the works. I had lost my virginity, like that. Boom.

"We broke up because he just did it. I had no say. Do you see what I mean? I told him I'd kill him if he told a soul."

Sounding academic and clinical in her approach, she paused, took a deep breath and said, "I think you, Charlie Jones, hold the key. You are the only way I am going to figure out what this is all about. It's like there is this big, dark secret of life out there that everyone is doing and no one wants us to find out about."

As she reached puberty, Susan had instinctively learned the pleasure of positioning herself under the running water of the bathtub. Despite her experience with Gene, the stir of those feelings and the erotic talks she and Charlie had been having were strong enough for her to suggest something she knew was wicked.

Chapter II

Love and War—Charlie's Parents

EVEN laid-back Venice, California, was buzzing with activity in 1942 after the declaration of war against Japan for the attack on the Pacific Fleet moored in Pearl Harbor. The soon-to-be Mr. and Mrs. Jones, the future parents of Charlie Jones, walked the long, wooden pier in silence. It was especially cool that night with a strong breeze coming in off the mighty Pacific Ocean.

The regular fishermen—wood tackle boxes, stringers and galvanized bait buckets—were at their familiar spots, casting down into the cold blue water that broke around the creosote pilings. Mesmerized by the sea below them, they only occasionally looked up and took notice of those passing.

Evett's arm was hooked through Ivory's who had both hands in the pockets of a tan corduroy jacket he liked to wear. Their shoulders were pulled in tight as they braced themselves against the damp chill of the wind. Like countless others whose lives and dreams were being upended by the war, they too had become victims.

Ivory had joined the Navy.

"I guess it was the right thing to do, querido."

"If it hadn't been for Pearl Harbor, I'd probably been forced into the infantry."

At their usual spot off to the side at the end of the pier, they propped their elbows on the railing and looked out into the darkness of the ocean and the night. The lights on the pier illuminating the water below obliterated any stars they might have been able to see.

"This way, if they get me, at least I've slept in a bed with sheets the night before."

"Bill, don't talk that way. Not even joking."

Donning a uniform to fight for truth, justice and the American way was a romantic notion held by most young men before they saw the reality of war, but not for Bill or Evett who were enamored with what they had been doing professionally.

Good attacking evil was certainly being glorified in

the hastily made movies coming out of Hollywood where William "Bill" "Ivory" Jones worked as a studio musician. Bill's nickname was "Ivory" because he *could* play the piano. Ever since he signed on at RKO Pictures, his name had appeared on the credits of dozens of movies. Granted, the credits moved quickly, but it was there, as was the regular paycheck.

Ivory was part of a small group of players who seemed otherworldly. With a brilliant knack for improvising and arranging, he was one of the best studio guys in the business. Before Hollywood, traveling the country with one band or another—country, swing, jazz, ragtime, blues—Bill "Ivory" Jones had been around the block a couple of times for someone 23-years-old, born and raised in Corpus Christi, Texas.

His credits included fill-in work with Glenn Miller, a summer with Benny Goodman and several gigs featuring Louis Armstrong. He'd jammed with Bob Wills and the Texas Playboys.

Traveling the country during the Great Depression made him appreciate his bi-weekly paycheck, which he considered large. But as poor as he and his fellow musicians had been while they were on the road, they weren't nearly as poor as a lot of people they'd seen milling around losing hope. Music seemed to be one of the few things that brought a smile to those beaten down, giving them a little twinkle in their eyes—some spunk.

Now, at the beginning of a promising musical career, in love, having more fun than he had ever had, making money, he was being told by his country to lay aside everything that meant anything to him and kill or be killed by people he knew about only through newspaper articles and newsreels.

Hitler and Nazi Germany had been dominating the news until, seemingly out of nowhere from the other side of the world, the Japanese had pulled their devastating surprise, December 7, 1941 attack on Pearl Harbor.

"Are your folks taking the plan any better?"

"Oh, Bill, they keep trying to hold on to their old-fashioned ways in a world that's turned upside down. They're trying to like you, honestly, they are. But, they want me to marry one of our own. It's not your fault that you're a 'gringo' and not Catholic. They think I never would have fallen in love with someone like you if I had stayed at home, away from Hollywood and the wild motion picture people. I will insist, and they'll agree, but right now they're trying to talk me out of the wedding until the war's over."

Fog was beginning to roll in, causing tiny crystals of moisture to catch in their hair and slightly moisten their faces.

Silent for a while, Ivory pulled a joint out of his pocket that they shared before he flicked the embers and put what was left back for later when they would drink young California wine and make love with the windows open.

Evett Bárbara, her stage name, was an up and coming "Mexican" actress. She had played the lead role in two successful Spanish films, and was an often-recognized celebrity in the Spanish speaking community of the United States and México.

It was Evett's genetic gift that turned heads wherever she went. A person simply could not not look at her. Tall with a marvelous figure, her intense dark eyes, with every look, told Ivory how much she loved him. He knew he was a lucky man.

Though Evett had a lot going for her, there were several things going against her. Carmen Miranda, the Brazilian Bombshell, "Chica Chica Boom Chic" with the hat made of tropical fruit, was the queen of Latina stars. Apparently, one queen was enough, leaving Evett with lower budget Mexican films, or housekeeper roles in the English pictures. A brutal occupation, especially for a woman, the casting couch wasn't a myth.

The war was another blow to her career. Virtually

every motion picture was now a patriotic movie. The typical soldier was the North American male leaving the stereo-typical true-blue American female to fight the mechanically fiendish German "Krauts" or the determined slant-eyed "Jap" bastards, depending on which side of the world the motion picture was dealing with.

For Ivory, the marching cadences were not what he enjoyed playing, but he was happy where he was. He sure didn't mind not having to deal with club managers, booking agents and constant travel.

It was all about to become moot anyhow, because Ivory was going to see the war firsthand, up close, where the airplanes weren't attached to the ground, and the pilots weren't given towels to wipe the fake grime and blood off their faces after the day's shoot.

Evett was sure about one thing. "You, my dear 'Ivory' Bill Jones, and I are going to see a priest. My parents will come around. I know they will. Even if they don't, I want a ring on your finger. You'll probably be stationed in Tahiti with nothing but half-naked women running around."

"What kind of name is this 'Ibory' Hones?" Evett's mother, María García, and father, José García, asked when she insisted on going through with the nuptials. "¿Como se dice 'Ibory Hones'? 'Ibory' es el diente del elefante, the tooth of the elephant, ¿Verdad? Bienvenidos, Diente del Elefante. I understand you want the hand of my daughter." At least her family could pronounce "Ibory" better than they could "Bill" which came out "Beell," or "William," which sounded like "Will-young." In Spanish the "J" in Jones is pronounced like an "H", which meant their little girl, their pride and joy, wanted to marry a young piano player named Will-young Beell Ibory Hones. "Mama, it's like Chile, dice Chones, okay Mama?"

It was bad enough that she had changed her name from Elena García to Evett Bárbara and taken up with the English-speaking crowd. That she wanted to marry one of them was not going over well. When Evett angrily insisted, her family reluctantly tried to act festive and appear happy during and after the "intimate" ceremony they had discouraged so adamantly.

And Ibory tried his hardest to fit in, to do and say the right things. Even her parents agreed that his Tex/Mex Spanish wasn't terrible. Language-wise, the problem Ivory had was with jokes. He could understand most of what was being said and was able to communicate in general conversation, but jokes could be confusing, and he'd laugh at the wrong time.

A good example of his bilingual deficiencies occurred during the reception at the García's home in East

L.A. In Spanish, aside from the group, her uncle said with a mischievous smile, "Ivory, you be good to my little niece or her papa will cook your 'Huevos'."

"Huevos" to Will-young meant eggs not testicles. Ivory thought the uncle was saying that Evett's father had taught her how to cook eggs. He hadn't the faintest idea why her uncle would find this amusing, but he obligingly laughed nonetheless. Evett still kidded him about it.

Newlyweds, the evening ritual of walking down the Venice pier two blocks from their rented home was profound—the Pacific Ocean looked vast and sinister the night before Ivory got on a gray Navy bus and headed for basic training.

The next day, standing at attention after having his hair cut off, etc., etc., 23-year-old Ivory felt like an out-of-place old-timer around the fresh 18-year-old recruits. As the weeks went on, his level of frustration was amplified by the fact that the only piano he could practice on was in the Navy chapel. For a bitter, honky-tonk, barroom piano player separated from his new bride, the "holy" atmosphere was a horrible prelude to being shipped off to fight in a terrible war. Even the piano felt like it would rather be playing "Onward, Christian Soldiers" than "St. Louis Blues."

At least during Ivory's initial naval training, he and

Evett were able to see each other occasionally. Never caught, he came awfully close more than once when he would sneak off base to spend part of the night with her. His fellow sailors were in awe of his clandestine courage and covered for him unfailingly.

Ivory's logic was, "If I get caught, they can throw me out or throw me in the brig, which couldn't be much worse than what I'm going through now." Anyway, John Wayne would have slugged down a shot of whiskey and done the same thing. Part of Ivory's mystique was that he personally knew John Wayne who enjoyed this irreverent piano player from South Texas.

Ivory's attitude was summed up by a bosun's mate who commented on something a sailor had done wrong— "That are dumb." Everything going on around him and what he was being trained to do "are dumb."

Tears streamed down the cheeks of mothers and wives as they saw the aircraft carrier *Enterprise,* with Ivory onboard, being pushed away from the dock by tugboats. Destination: classified. It was understood that wherever they went, it was to engage the enemy. Tears rolled down the cheeks of quite a few sailors and their fathers, too, because, despite government claims to the contrary, the war was not going all that well.

Transitioning from a depressed, peacetime economy to an all-out war effort was much more difficult and time consuming than had been optimistically predicted. By late 1942 there was no end in sight, whatsoever. For the U.S., the war was really just beginning when the *Enterprise* sailed out of the harbor with Ivory as part of the "ground" crew. On the flight deck, his job was to get the pilots into their planes and help get the fighters into position for take-off.

The first two weeks at sea were uneventful. Like the calm before the storm, the Pacific Ocean was exceptionally beautiful on the day that all hell did break loose. At first, everyone thought it was another drill when the alarms sounded full alert. Like a disturbed ant bed, sailors rapidly erupted from within the ship and rushed to their battle stations. Then, from behind an innocent looking white cumulus cloud formation, dozens of single-engine Jap fighters came raining down upon them.

The noise was astonishing—deafeningly loud. Nothing Ivory had been taught in basic training or seen on a Hollywood set came even close to the screaming RPM of enemy engines, the rapid fire of wing-mounted machine guns and the even louder sound of the ship's cannon and anti-aircraft guns as the ship blasted away at Japanese A6M "Zeros" made by Mitsubishi. Adding to the horrific explosions was the roar of the *Enterprise's* F6F Hellcat

Fighters taking off as alarms continuously rang, and then ... there was silence, total silence....

As Ivory slowly came to, the first sound he was aware of was the familiar droning of the ship's mammoth diesel engines. As his head cleared, he began hearing sounds of those waiting for death or the operating table.

"What's going on?" he quietly asked a sailor grimacing next to him.

"We're floating, and we're under our own power. We were able to mount a counterattack the 'old man' believes was enough to keep them off our backs for a while. It's like a game of cat and mouse. Somewhere out there, not far from us, is an enemy convoy about the same size ours is."

Ivory's head, his left hand and his leg, were bandaged. He could feel his fingers underneath the bandage and that was a relief. He couldn't move his foot, which was bad, but it was a hell of a lot better than the agony of sailors looking at missing arms and legs or trying to see through bandaged eyes. Because his wounds were not life threatening, it was 20-plus hours before Ivory found out about nature's cruel trick.

Chapter III

Jones' Lumber and Hardware

FEELING insignificant below the gigantic warship, Evett, along with her mother and father, had been waiting for hours on the large cement dock, when they spotted Ivory on a stretcher being carried through a gray door located well below the flight deck of the *Enterprise.*

All she could do was hold his good hand for the few moments she was allowed to walk beside him. Looking weak, he tried but couldn't say much other than, "It'll be okay," in that soft Texas drawl. Evett and her parents were told to go to the waiting room when they took him inside the hospital for admission and processing.

Because casualties were classified information,

Evett had no idea how severe the wounds were until a pal of his from the ship using one of Bill's photographs found her in the crowded waiting room.

Stepping outside, "Ma'am, he's going to be all right. I promised him I'd find you and tell you he's okay. He's going to make it," said the farm boy from Minnesota who looked like a child with rosy cheeks and Swedish blue eyes.

"Mrs. Jones, I hate to be the one to tell you, but his left hand was hurt pretty bad. The leg's going to be okay in a while. Ma'am, me and the guys, we're afraid he won't be to be able to play the piano the way he used to." Trying to reassure Evett he went on, "Your husband is a hell of ... I'm sorry, we've been at sea a long time, a heck of a man." Taking a breath, the youngster was anxious to talk, but was having trouble in the presence of a woman, especially this woman so close to him.

Luckily, the war was over for her husband. The shipmates who had been close to Ivory were both envious and sad for him. They were glad that he was home for good and sad because they felt that Ivory Jones was, from that infamous moment on, going to be known as just plain Bill Jones. The inescapable conclusion was, you can't play the piano with eight-and-a half-fingers.

Soon after arriving at the hospital in San Diego, Bill could take the bus to their Venice apartment where they again walked the long pier, albeit slower with Ivory on crutches. Rules and regulations were loose for wounded sailors.

"What do you think we should do?" Evett asked her unusually quiet husband.

"We've got some options. Did you read the letters from Dad?"

Evett nodded, afraid to bring up "options" because she feared it would further aggravate Bill, who was in a dark place. Yet in this tragic turmoil, there was a huge burden off his and Evett's shoulders. He was alive, and he wouldn't have to go back to a war that was just getting revved up.

The worst part was running into old buddies and looking at their faces when they saw the left hand in a cast. It was a musical death, and music was all he knew. It was all he cared about. He didn't know what to do or how to handle it.

At the same time, Evett's agent was having a terrible time getting decent acting parts.

So it was at the end of the Venice pier, they made the emotional, terribly difficult decision to pack their belongings and go to Corpus Christi, Texas, where at least temporarily Bill could help his father run the lumberyard that bore the family name—Jones' Lumber and Hardware.

Barely able to keep the doors open and food on the table during the Depression, the wartime economy had papa Jones' lumber business jumping. He sorely needed help.

"Evett, it seems like ages ago that I got on that train to Houston—Mom and Dad at the train station waving goodbye. They looked so small and bewildered, wondering where they had gone wrong as they looked at the train windows trying to find me. All I wanted to do was see the world and play the piano. New York, L.A., nightclubs, stage lights, action, that was the life for me. I couldn't wait to get away from south Texas. The last thing I wanted to do was work at a small-town lumberyard. It won't be easy for either of us, especially you. If this world ever gets itself straightened out...."

Since his eventual discharge was a foregone conclusion, he was able to get a transfer to the Navy base in Corpus that could perform the next surgery on his leg. The Navy no longer had any use for him, and it freed up a much-needed hospital bed on the West Coast.

It was, by far, the most painful decision Evett had ever faced or thought she would ever have to face, and it was on her mind every waking hour. She would be leaving her family, her entire *familia*, moving *far* away. She could be giving up her career as a motion picture actress. Puta guerra, maybe when it was over and things returned to normal they could return as he had promised.... Deep down she felt, probably not.

Tearfully, Bill and Evett said goodbye to family and friends. Unable to move most of their possessions, they sold or gave away what they couldn't put in suitcases. With war restrictions, just arranging transportation to Corpus wasn't easy. Nothing was easy hobbling around on crutches with a bum hand. On the service bulletin board, Evett found three Navy wives who needed a fourth and a fifth rider to make the trip eastward. Their husbands were being transferred to Corpus Christi, and the only way they could make the trip was to find two additional riders so they could pool gas rationing stamps.

One last time, on the cool coast of California, a gloriously naked Evett lowered herself onto her husband with casts on his hand and leg. One of those last moments in Venice was the minuscule beginning of Charlie Jones, something they wouldn't know until a month after they arrived in Texas.

It was a long drive on two-lane, state roads in a car without air conditioning. The only relief from the heat was the triangle windows on the driver's and passenger's side that funneled air into the Packard where Bill and Evett became close with these sailors' wives as they crossed the tumbleweed deserts of Arizona and New Mexico. There was also a vent in front of the windshield that allowed some air flow. Still, it was so damn hot they splurged on a motel room in Tucson with AC where the group rested up for the night drive to a furnace called El Paso. There again they chipped in for a room, had a good Mexican meal across the border and bought three 50-cent bottles of rum to help them get through Fort Stockton, Bakersfield and Ozona. In front of them, on the endless highway was an ever-beckoning mirage of what appeared to be water distorted by heat rising from the black asphalt. Unreachable, it was always just ahead of them.

Occasionally, they would pass a car or pickup truck.

The skin underneath Bill's casts sweated and itched like crazy. Even more uncomfortable were several snide remarks overheard along the way about the soldier married to the good-lookin' "spic."

L.A. was hip, it was cool, so nothing much was said about a "white" being married to a Mexican. Sometimes, they were stared at by tourists, but that was all. Everyone who had known them in California didn't think twice about it—everyone except Evett's family. They were still having trouble with the fact that their oldest, most beautiful daughter had married a gringo whose name they couldn't pronounce. Now she was on her way to Texas with "elephant tooth" who was crippled.

Finally pulling into Corpus Christi, Evett was relieved to see a town that wasn't as bad as some of the ones they'd been driving through, which wasn't saying much. For a while during their automobile odyssey, she felt as though they were driving on the moon. Thank God the Packard hadn't broken down as it labored over the Great Divide and the deserts between the West Coast and the Gulf of Mexico.

Looking out of the open automobile window as they entered town, the baked greens weren't near the greens of California. Shrubs in the dried front yards were nothing compared to the magnificent plants, flowers and lawns on the West Coast and the surrounding hills. With the exception of two hotels downtown and several Victorian homes on the bluff, everything was short and square. Compared to the cold blue of the Pacific Ocean, the chocolate milk colored bay water was just plain ugly. Ivory knew what Corpus looked like, but to Evett everything looked dull and hick. It was not an easy time for the mother-to-be who, except for México, had never been out of the state of California. At that moment, the color that came to mind describing Corpus Christi, "el cuerpo de Jesus," was puppy-shit brown—caca.

Unable to drive because he couldn't depress the

clutch, Bill directed the young traveling companion to his parent's home where they hugged and said goodbyes, promising to stay in touch as their suitcases were unloaded. On a straight cement walkway in the middle of a barren lawn, Bill Jones introduced Frank and Betty Jones to his bride, Evett Bárbara Jones.

Luckily, through family connections the couple was able to find a duplex for rent. Upstairs, there were two bedrooms. Downstairs was the living room, a dining area and the kitchen. But, the best part was the screened-in front porch that always had a breeze blowing through. Located on Cole Street, they were two short blocks from Cole Park on the Corpus Christi shoreline.

Setting up house helped take her mind off things, but these were extremely difficult months for Latina Evett. She did not know a single person, nor did they know her, and they all looked and dressed remarkably alike. Adding to the confusion, the layout of Corpus is not logical. Ivory's family, the business and the paper map his mom marked so she could get from one place to another, like the grocery store, were all that saved her until the baby came. Initially, Ivory's parents loaned them one of their cars until they were able to buy a green 1942 Chevrolet Special DeLuxe Fleetline. The lumber business was doing well.

Eight months after their frazzled arrival, on the

second floor of Corpus Christi's Spohn Hospital, Evett gave birth to a healthy baby boy they named Charlie García Jones. C.G.J. were the initials he would eventually emboss on his briefcase.

The hectic pace of the lumber business by day, Evett and baby Charlie at night, helped Bill keep his mind off his missing fingers. Struggling on the piano, he could have acted depressed—he was. He could have moped around making his life and the lives of those around him miserable, but he consciously decided that wasn't what he wanted to do.

In a morbid way, the letter he'd opened one morning from a shipmate helped. A pilot Ivory had been close to on the *Enterprise* had died when his F6F Hellcat burst into flames. Coming back from a mission, the crippled airplane had hit the deck too hard just as the ship was rising from an unusually large swell. Ivory could see it—extinguish the fire, push the charred plane and the charred pilot over the side into the ocean as fast as possible so the rest of the squadron could land.

Lying in bed under a single sheet with a fan blowing across him and Evett, when everyone was asleep and the neighborhood was quiet, he thought about his lot in life and decided he would just have to make the best of the hand he had been dealt. The recurring nightmare of the

Japanese attack replaying his personal tragedy only reinforced the fact that he was still alive with a wife, and now, a son.

The ship's surgeon had done a good job of closing Ivory's wound so the scar wasn't grotesque. Two weeks after moving into an apartment, when the casts were taken off, he had a noticeable limp and muscle atrophy, but that gradually disappeared.

At the lumberyard, behind the counter, Bill put up a sign that read:

WARNING!
DO NOT MAKE ME MAD,
I'M ALMOST OUT OF HAND AS IT IS!

Bill's father had learned long ago that funny signs on the wall were good for business. As short-handed as he had been before Bill's arrival, customers were sometimes going to have to wait, and they did so a lot better if they were entertained by corny philosophy on the wall.

THE MORE YOU COMPLAIN
THE LONGER GOD LETS YOU STAY ON EARTH

As soon as Bill and Evett were settled into the

wood-frame duplex rental, Bill bought a Baldwin Upright Piano for $25. Sounding depressingly thin, he needed to figure out a way to play the bass lines with the missing little finger and the stub of a ring finger. After experimenting with several contraptions, he inserted a splint into a glove, the slightly curved type used to immobilize a broken finger and stuffed it with cotton. Then he cut the ends off the remaining glove fingers. Within a matter of weeks, he was again able to "boogie woogie." "Ivory" was back in business, and the evenings came alive.

One of the many signs in the lumberyard said:

THE RICH MAY HAVE ALL THE MONEY
BUT THE POOR HAVE ALL THE FUN

Air conditioning was years away from sealing people from their neighbors, so a pleasantly pungent sea breeze from the Gulf of Mexico and Corpus Christi Bay kept the gathering of people at the Jones' home comfortable. It would be 1950 before television came along. Why listen to the radio, when Ivory's fake finger was hitting the low notes?

With the heat of the day behind them, while children ran around playing made-up games and catching fireflies; friends, neighbors, navy wives (including their cross-country driving buddies), homesick sailors and men too old to fight, sang North American and Mexican songs until they were exhausted and the children had to be put to bed. The icebox was always filled with cold Carta Blanca beer. Tamales, jalapeño cornbread and beans were on the stove. For Bill "Ivory" Jones and his wife, Evett Jones, things were not too terrible, considering.

For those in the neighborhood hoping their lover or brother would return safely, a night at the Jones' could, for a little while anyhow, make a person forget about the war and the loneliness that made hearts ache for those who had gone overseas to fight and perhaps die.

Chapter IV

Perpetual Motion

THIS was the sinful arrangement Susan and Charlie clandestinely made. When they got the opportunity, they would take their clothes off together. Promising with all their hearts, their sacred, secret meeting would take place only once, they vowed *they would never, never, ever, ever tell a soul. No second thoughts. No confessions.* As long as they didn't get caught, no one would ever know.

Arranging the meeting was not as difficult as they first thought it would be. Opportunity presented itself the following week when Susan's parents left town for a banking convention. Though Susan was staying with a girlfriend while they were gone, she had a key to the house so she could take out the garbage, collect the mail and keep an eye on things in general.

After checking the pronunciation in a dictionary, Charlie went to a drugstore on the other side of town to ask the pharmacist for a package of Trojan "prophylactics."

Wednesday evening, a school night, she told her host family she needed to go by the house and then to the downtown library for an hour or so—back around 9, 9:30.

Driving in silence in her car, not knowing what to say, Charlie, as a precaution, ducked down as they turned the corner and parked in the carport of her home on Catalina Place Drive. After Susan got out and opened the side door to the house that led to the kitchen, he snuck inside. The Duncan's house was typical suburban Corpus Christi, a one-story brick home with wood-shingle roof. The living room had white carpet and there was a fireplace in the family room where a black and white patterned sofa sat in between two chrome chairs with black cushions. The seating arrangement faced their built-in color television set on the wood-paneled wall.

After an awkward pause, Susan went to the kitchen cabinet and made them a stiff rum and coke before she motioned for him to follow as they took their drinks down the hallway to her bedroom where she turned on the lamp beside the bed.

It was weird for Charlie to be in such teenage feminine surroundings. Everything was girlie. The bed they sat on had a white canopy, and the pillowcases were trimmed with white lace. Four fluffy pillows were arranged neatly against the white headboard.

"Should I kiss you?" Charlie asked as they awkwardly sat down on the edge of the bed. They had kissed only once before and that was when their lips had brushed in the sixth grade.

"No, I don't think so," she said with tears beginning to form in her eyes. "I think you should just go ahead and take 'em off, your pants, Charlie. I'm frightened too, I'll turn away if you want."

Charlie and Susan both took big gulps of the rum and coke before he, in the dim light, slipped off his shoes and socks, then his Levis and finally his underwear. She unbuttoned his shirt and slipped it off his broad shoulders exposing a tight stomach and young man with a real hard, dangerous looking erection.

"Oh my, Charlie ... Incredible, Charlie, absolutely incredible."

They both looked down at what looked like a tall mushroom, sinister and evil as she studied the veins and lightly touched its sides causing Charlie to suck air.

"Look Charlie. Charlie, your balls keep moving around even when you're sitting still. Look at them." They reminded her of a perpetual motion liquid lava lamp. It was funny, and, for the first time, they smiled at each other.

"I guess it's my turn."

Reaching for the first button of her blouse, unbuttoning it, taking the blouse off her shoulders and pulling her arms through the sleeves, reaching behind her back and unhooking her brassiere: there they were—a young woman's breasts—her pale, hard nipples were pointing right at him. Awkwardly, he put the palm of his hand over one.

They talked, looked and gently touched before he took one of the condoms out of his wallet and put it on.

Very gentle at first, both were in new territory when Susan's back tightly arched and her pelvis jerked involuntarily. She gasped when he eventually withdrew and rolled over onto his back next to her.

Snuggling next to him, she saw what he looked like when it wasn't in the moment. No longer sinister and threatening, she thought it looked rather cute when it wasn't causing trouble. Still sensitive, Charlie flinched slightly as he took off the sperm laden latex. Susan took it from him with two fingers and put it on the nightstand before she covered their naked bodies with the sheet.

"You look really funny in this bed," she smiled, and he did with the white frills around his chest where she snuggled against him and put her head on his shoulder. "This is pretty wild, Charlie. This could cause problems." Neither had ever held someone of the opposite sex naked and it felt uncomfortably good, better than good. "I suppose we have our own little problem, like what are we going to do now."

She didn't feel guilty—she felt snug, warm and safe with her bare leg over him.

Should he ask her to marry him? He knew it was supposed to be an experiment, but that was before, and this was now. Should he tell her he loved her? He should at least tell the girl who had blushingly shown him her clitoris that he loved her.

"I love you, Susan."

"It's okay Charlie, relax, it's all right. You're a great guy to put up with me. Boy, we had a lot to talk about before this. I had no idea."

Susan got up, went to the bathroom and closed the door. She came back with a warm washcloth causing him to begin stiffening again.

"Down boy," Susan smiled as she put on fresh panties and cutoffs. When they were both dressed, he helped her tidy the room and bed so it wouldn't look as though two hormone ravaged teenagers had just had orgasms.

"You men are kind of hairy, you know," she said before she hit the switch on a vacuum cleaner that sucked the bed clean.

Susan couldn't resist picking up the used condom and putting her finger inside to see what the fluid felt and looked like—creamy, milky, sticky with an unusual odor, not unpleasant—different.

While Charlie stayed out of view, Susan put the trash container with the damning evidence wrapped in paper towels on the curb out front. Certain everything was as it should be, Charlie quickly got into the passenger side and lowered his head so he couldn't be seen as they drove away.

Once clear, Charlie looked over at Susan's silhouette as she concentrated on the road, "I don't know what to say."

Coming to a stop by his car, Susan eyes sparkled as she looked into his, "You did good tonight, really good, Charlie." Putting her hand on his arm, "I will never forget the first time I really, truly made love. Now get going or I'm going to be in trouble."

The visions Charlie had running through his mind

wouldn't go away as he pulled into the driveway of his family's Southern California Spanish-Style house with a terracotta roof, ceiling fans and open windows.

Corpus Christi was exceptionally beautiful the spring of Susan and Charlie's senior year—the year of the tryst. It was also a time for both to make big decisions about their future away from home, and they talked about it a lot. Recruited by several schools, Charlie decided to go to the University of Texas where he had been offered a full scholarship to play football. Susan, though she thought about UT, chose to go to Southern Methodist University, a smaller school where her parents had gone.

As part of the class of 1961, wearing red caps and gowns, they graduated from W.B. Ray High School in a ceremony that began with the school fight song:

> We are the fighting Texans
> Stalwart and upright fellows
> We'll meet the foe in combat
> Never say die we'll fight, fight, fight, fight
> With all our silver powers
> And all the scarlet in our veins
> We will fight with all our might
> To do the foe up right
> And bring home a victory

Their eyes met as she received her diploma and they smiled.

But, before leaving and with even more astonishing results, they did see each other in the biblical sense three more times despite their solemn promise not to. Both felt they were making a mature decision by agreeing not to go to the same school because they, undoubtedly, would become sex maniacs and who knows what would happen. Their lives were just beginning.

At the end of summer, Charlie carefully loaded the used Chevrolet Ivory had bought for him to drive to Austin. His shirts hung neatly from a bar that spanned the back seat.

That same morning, Susan and her dad crammed seven large suitcases into her new Buick Skylark convertible for the drive to Dallas.

Charlie followed her as far as Austin where they pulled over at a Texaco station to say goodbye. Between the gas pump and her car, they hugged and kissed several soft kisses. With the top down, scarf waving in the wind, Charlie thought she looked awfully pretty as he watched her disappear down the highway.

Chapter V
Hal, Red, and Oil Wells

HAL was originally from Cuero, Texas (pop. 7,338), and Red was originally from Goliad, Texas (pop. 1,782)—nothing towns in the middle of nowhere on State Road 183. During the Texas Revolution, the battle cry for the soon-to-be Lone Star State was, "Remember the Alamo!" "Remember Goliad!" As time marched on, people did remember the Alamo, but forgot all about Goliad.

Hal's dad had been a traveling farm equipment salesman who came home less and less until he quit showing up at all. To augment his mother's salary as a bank teller at First National, she began taking in boarders at their two-story home on the San Antonio River on the outskirts of town.

As it turned out, most of the men who stayed in her dormitory-style sleeping quarters were oil men—a revolving group of roughnecks, surveyors, petroleum engineers, drill bit salesmen, well-monitoring company representatives, etc. Hal Burton's mom, provided them with a bed, an occasional meal and kitchen privileges.

In her backyard, under the shade trees by the river, there was a picnic table and four contoured metal outdoor chairs where folks could sit down after a hard day's work and have a few ice-cold beers. Mrs. Burton had two every evening—doctor's orders—two Pearl Beers brewed in San Antonio with water from the country of 1,100 springs. Her favorite country star, Ferlin Husky, told her over the radio how good it tasted, and they did.

As a child, Hal loved the stories, the bitching and moaning about the cheap son-of-a-bitch owner, the jackass of a tool-pusher or the lazy driller. He'd heard so many of them, when he got his first job as a roughneck at 16, he felt as though he was on familiar ground. For Hal, the oil rig symbolized everything the state of Texas stood for—power, fuel, heavy industry, progress—if there's a job to be done, just do it—and, of course, there was oil money.

In the tin shed beside the rig, where they took off their street clothes and put on gray work jumpsuits, Hal would pull off his cowboy boots and pull on his metal-toed work boots along with the other hard-working men with pale bodies and leather faces.

His first job was on a medium-large rig powered by three Waukesha 12-cylinder diesel engines that were taller than a man. For a while, they called him "Weevil"—short for boll weevil—which is what a rookie's called until he's a real roughneck.

The single most difficult job on an oil rig is making a "round trip." When a drill bit wears out, all the pipe has to be pulled out of the ground so a new one can be put on. If the hole is shallow, a round trip is no big deal but when the bit is 12,000 feet or more below the earth's surface, that's another story. To pull two miles of heavy pipe out of the ground took all three diesels working a block and tackle with an eight-to-one purchase.

>Born to be a roughneck
>I'll never amount to nothing
>Pulling case and laying pipe
>It's hard labor
>
>I learned to cuss when I was two
>And fight when I was three
>By the time I was five

There was no kid alive
'Could ever get the best of me

I remember walkin' down the road
When I heard somebody say
He was born to a roughneck's life
And he's never going to change his ways

    Those were the words to a country song written and sung by Johnny Cash that sent chills up Hal's spine every time he heard it on the radio.

    When a well came in or was declared dry, one of the last steps was to lower the derrick using the rig's own cable. Afterwards, for the first time in perhaps months, the diesel engines were shut down and all was eerily quiet including the immediate countryside. A trucking crew would come in, load the big rig onto flatbed trailers and move it to its new location.

    Hal was saving every penny he could because he was ready to gamble.

    On charts, he researched and marked where every live well was and where every dry hole had been. But, even more important than his self-taught geological knowledge, Hal was lucky and intuitive. A hundred-and-fifty yards from a dry hole could be a pool of oil large enough to make someone rich.

Hal and Red met one Saturday night in a country beer joint halfway between Cuero and Goliad in a "wet" county-line bar in the countryside. In Texas there are always counties that vote "wet" bordering the ones that vote dry. Wearing a snap-up country-western shirt with several unsnapped, her jeans were so tight he didn't know how she could have gotten into them. Or from his perspective, how he could get her out of them. Not much of a dancer, after a few beers, he was ready to give anything a try to meet this honky-tonk angel with flaming red hair. He wasn't the only bird dog on the hunt, either.

The bar itself was a broken-down, cigarette smoke-filled building underneath a sagging roof. Window air conditioners laboring in the walls accompanied the five-piece country band made up of four farm boys and one cowboy's sweetheart.

In Texas, before bars were legally allowed to sell liquor by the drink, if they were in a county that voted "wet," they could sell beer, wine and "set-ups"—a glass of ice and a Coke or 7UP for the people who bring their own bottles, which was legal. Long neck beer bottles, hard liquor bottles in paper bags and glasses filled with ice and plastic swizzle-sticks littered the tables as the couples did the two-step across the only dance floor within miles.

Hal drove Red home that night, and they talked in the car for over an hour before she went inside the house where she lived with her mom and dad. Turns out her mom was a beautician at Bobby's Beauty Salon (and gossip center). Her dad was a mailman, and she worked at the Sears and Roebuck catalog outlet. Red only half-jokingly told him that among the three of them they had a pretty good idea about the goings-on in town. Keeping her ears open at the dinner table, Red learned the world wasn't always as it seemed.

Red's red hair had come to Texas directly from Ireland via Oklahoma where Red's red-headed mother met and eloped with her dad, winding up in Goliad where they figured correctly, they wouldn't be found. Her family—Irish Catholics fleeing the Great Potato Famine—were treated so miserably and miserly after their arrival at New York's Ellis Island, they joined the thousands that traveled west for the Great Oklahoma Land Rush of 1889. At high noon on April 22, the cannon sounded. Over 50,000 people who had been waiting at the Oklahoma border cracked their whips and dug in their spurs, looking to claim land. Oklahoma City on the morning of the 22nd had a population of a few dozen. A day later, the population was 10,000 and growing.

Red's parents staked their claim in a city named

Tulsa, which is where she would meet her future husband.

The uncomfortable truth was that the waves of Europeans who migrated to America were, for the most part, not their finest. Generally speaking, a large portion were outcasts and religious fanatics—tough and cruel people that braved the Atlantic to begin a new life in a new country.

The long and short of it was, when the two fell in love, they knew they would have to run away because he was from a fire and brimstone Baptist family, and she was from an Irish Catholic family. They would never be allowed to marry—never.

So, on the night of a new moon in the cover of darkness, they saddled one of the two horses belonging to her parents. On the kitchen table, they left money for the horse and a note explaining why they were eloping—with one big lie they never regretted. They said they were going north to Chicago when they were really heading south into a new unknown—the state of Texas—where they found and settled in a small town called Goliad.

Feeling butterflies, Red and Hal kissed goodnight before he began the drive back to Cuero and Red quietly opened the screen door and tiptoed inside.

Hal didn't look much different than the other boys hanging out on a Saturday night—boots, jeans, flowered cowboy shirts, Old Spice cologne—until he started talking about where there might be some oil—the ultimate game of hide-'n'-seek. It was pure, it was complicated, the variables were everywhere, and yet there were patterns. On the surface, there may be rows of cotton or corn, but below there were formations filled with black gold, if you could find it.

For a "wildcatter," which Hal was hoping to become, it was the ultimate poker game with nature saying, "You are going to have to pay a lot of money and drill deep to see if I've got what you're looking for." For Red, who wanted more than Dairy Queen dinners and jukebox love, Hal came off as a person with ambition that was bigger than hot air on a barstool. Plus, he had a good job and money in the bank.

Eight months after a night at Eddie Brown's hotel, they were married at the First Baptist Church of Cuero.

Anyone from a big city would laugh at the long tables and folding metal chairs set up under the large oak tree behind the church, but weddings are serious affairs in these small Texas towns. Baptists didn't drink or dance so the men with weathered faces, "V"-tanned necks and white heads from wearing hats in the sun, talked about crops and drilling rigs. In clusters, women wearing their Sunday dresses talked about how lovely the bride and groom looked.

After a two-night honeymoon in San Antonio, they moved into their first home—a trailer at the end of a dirt road on 95 acres of grazing land that they shared with cows, cow shit, trees and a windmill that kept the water trough full.

They were so in love there weren't enough hours in the day for each other, literally. As time and their two-year anniversary passed, the monotony of Red's life began wearing on her. She needed Hal at home in their bed at night. As things stood, she didn't mind working five days a week, 9 to 5 at Sears, but Hal was gone all the time on out-of-town rig locations. When he was home, he was distracted with errands, charts, maps and telephone calls.

For Red, going to work, coming home alone to a trailer out in a cow pasture where there was nothing to do but listen to the radio and reread Hollywood magazines—*she drank a shot of Beam*—was not what she had signed up for. No siree. Goddamnit, this was Friday night.

She made a stiff bourbon-and-seven for the drive, put on her jeans, snap-up shirt, cowboy hat and boots, grabbed the pint and headed to a new dance hall she'd heard about, that was not unlike where she and Hal had met except that it was on the other side of town, further down the road. *It was okay to flirt with danger. She was a strong woman. She could handle it. If there was one thing she could do, it was handle men.*

ROY'S LONGHORN BALLROOM is where she slowdanced with a man who would change her life in a radical and unforeseen way. *It's only dancing.*

Having finished the pint of Jim Beam, not ready to go home at closing time, she let herself get talked into going outside and into the industrial van of the handsome young blond Snap-On tool salesman she'd been dancing with to share his bottle. *One nightcap before hitting the road.*

Inside the roomy truck with chrome wrenches hanging on the walls, they talked about things she couldn't remember, flirted—*it's okay to flirt a little*— before he leaned over and kissed her. *She'd let him kiss her once.* With only slight hesitation, Red draped her arms around his neck and tilted her head so his tongue could more easily slide inside her mouth. She was so lonely and burning from his touch that felt tender, warm and good.

He clamped his hand firmly on her rear end, fingers almost in between her legs, as he pulled her close so she could feel what was in his jeans.

Letting him unsnap the top of her shirt, he cupped her breast then lowered his head to kiss its nipple. *She should stop him now. Now was the time to stop. She didn't want him to stop.*

Instead, on fire, she watched him unsnap the lower part of her shirt and slip it off her shoulders while she massaged his crotch.

As Snap-On began to undo his belt and Red stepped back to undo her jeans ... she couldn't get the *fucking button out of its slot.* Fumbling, in a hurry, she glanced up at the person who was now dropping his pants —maybe it was a headlight from the highway or maybe it was a flash in her mind—whatever it was, she saw this man that she had never met before on top of her, in and out of her. The most intimate of all human contact, he would still be on her....

Head spinning. *Whore. Hal.*

Panicked, unsteady, panicked, Red jerked as she flung her arm across her chest. There wasn't much light inside the van, only that from a blue sign on the highway that faintly flashed through the rear window. Even so, she could see his erection, brown scrotum and blond pubic hair.

Grabbing her hat and bag, she lunged out of the door almost falling as she pulled her shirt up from around her waist as best she could. It was dark. She, stumbling and afraid, started throwing up.

Off balance-running, half-walking across the empty

parking lot, vomiting bile, booze and bits of hard-boiled egg that splattered her boots and jeans, she kept rushing toward her car that was parked off to the side.

Had she looked back she would have seen his outline standing in the truck's doorway naked from the waist down except for his socks, but she didn't as she peeled out and hit the blacktop.

With dried tears on her cheeks, smelling like puke, she drove through the full-moon night on an empty highway, her shirt still unbuttoned to her navel. Close to home, raindrops from a squall began hitting the windshield as she drove the last hundred yards to their trailer at a quarter past two.

Under the front porch overhang as the thunderstorm blew rain in through the screen, Red scrubbed and washed her vomit covered boots, put her clothes in the washtub and lowered herself into a hot bath. Alarm set for seven o'clock, she slipped between the sheets of her bed. *Holy fucking shit.* What had she done? Oh my, Lord.

Early the next morning, feeling awful, madder than she'd ever been at herself, Red washed her hair, poured eye-drops into her eyes and with an unsteady hand put on makeup as best she could before driving to the grocery store where she acted the part of an early-to-rise housewife.

"Mornin' Mrs. Burton, fine weather we're having wouldn't you say."

"Yes, it is a fine mornin' Miss Wilson."

Three days later, shopping at the local pharmacy, she thought she was going to die of a heart attack right there in the drug store.

Hal was finally, really, due home that evening and, as she was picking up a bottle of Listerine and some toothbrushes, in walks Mr. Snap-On himself, wearing his work uniform.

Through the pharmacy window she could see the dreaded white, yellow and red truck where she'd let him kiss her, feel her and see her. *Oh my fucking God.* To avoid him, she turned to the rotating bookrack in the corner and grabbed what turned out to be a Harlequin novel even though she hadn't read a book in years.

Handsome and sure of himself, "What's your name, good-lookin'?"

She made sure he saw the ring. "I'm on my way home," she hissed through clenched teeth as she glanced down at the hand that had been inside her blouse and the slight bulge of the dick she had touched through his clothes.

"Lucky him." Mr. Snap-On said and quizzically checked her out again from head to toe and in between as he watched her pay for the book, toothbrushes and mouthwash.

"Wasn't that you at Roy's the other night?" he said, following her outside.

"Nope," she said as she quickly opened the driver side door, got in and slammed it shut.

From that day on Red started reading at night. She became a Harlequin romantic novel addict. They were all over the trailer. One night, after bitching at Hal again for being gone too much, he irritably and off-handedly said, "Hell, if this next one comes in, I'll buy my own damn rig, and we'll call it Harlequin Oil. I'll grow my hair long, bleach it like the pretty boys on the covers and drive you crazy hanging around the house all day long."

Lo and behold, it did come in, and it was the beginning of Harlequin Oil and Gas. The name had a good ring to it they thought—a lucky ring considering the money that began rolling in. Then and there at that moment in their lives, everything changed.

Hal still had to travel quite a bit, but he made Red quit her job at Sears so she could come along with him. Mornings she'd hunt for wild game in the surrounding country then sit in the trailer that followed the rig, feet propped up next to the air conditioner of the Harlequin Oil & Gas trailer, reading her latest Harlequin.

It was "on-site" that she became pregnant with the first of two redheaded boys.

Chapter VI

Business and Pleasure

SUSAN Duncan Richardson called Charlie at his law office on the 11th floor of the Driscoll Building in "Uptown" Corpus Christi, on the bluff. Once a grand hotel built by Mrs. Driscoll, it was now office space. The story goes that the extremely wealthy Mrs. Driscoll (who saved the Alamo) was so upset with the White Plaza Hotel that she followed through on her promise to build a hotel next door tall enough that she could piss on her neighbor.

Originally, the lobby of the Driscoll Hotel was extremely ornate. A marvelous black marble Art Deco entrance led to a lobby with substantial pink Italian marble columns, a gilded concert grand piano, rich imported carpets, French Rococo furniture and dramatic dueling curved stairways that led to an exotic mezzanine and framed the entrance to the Morocco Room. European elegance right there in uptown Corpus Christi.

Unfortunately, when the building eventually changed hands, the new owners gutted the lobby and covered the exterior with small black rectangular tiles—the kind that might be used for the outside walls of a strip mall or doctor's building and turned it into office space. Luckily for them, the regal Mrs. Driscoll was dead when the changes were made or the person responsible for the new decor would surely have been pissed on repeatedly.

"Mr. Jones, a Susan Richardson, she said she used to be Susan Duncan, is on the line."

Charlie had read about the death of Susan's husband and thought about calling her several times. Had he known what to say, he would have.

John Richardson was changing a flat tire in broad daylight on Highway 59 near Victoria, Texas, when the driver of a Ford F 1000 Super Duty semi-truck pulling a red trailer loaded with cabbage dozed off at the wheel and plowed into Richardson doing approximately 75 to 80 miles an hour. The newspapers duly reported that finding Richardson's remains had been difficult because, "due to the violent impact, cabbage and body parts were scattered over an area approximately the size of a football field. A roofing nail was found in the tire Mr. Richardson was attempting to change. He is survived by his wife of less than a year, Susan Richardson, his parents, Mr. and Mrs. John Richardson, and his two sisters, Kitty and Mary Anne Richardson."

"Can I see you, Charlie? I've got to get out of the house."

He leaned back in the leather chair behind his mahogany desk and thought about what she must be going through. It had been four years since they had seen each other briefly in passing, and he counted back 12 years since their high school rendezvous in her bedroom.

"Charlie, I know you're sorry. What I don't want now is someone who's sorry for me. I've given most of his clothes away. His parents wanted a lot of his things to remind them of him. It's been worse than awful.

"He was their only son. Everyone, especially my parents, feel so sorry for me, I think I might go berserk. Take me out to dinner, will you, Charlie? Let me meet you someplace dark where we can talk, and I can drink too much."

Later that evening, Susan took a cab to Mac's, an out-of-the-way Bar & Grill specializing in poor-boy sandwiches, mesquite grilled ribs and deep-fried red snapper.

She looked around for Charlie in the dimly lit cafe with miniature jukeboxes mounted on the walls in between the vinyl covered booths.

He was in the back, in the corner.

Sliding in opposite him, she took off the old baseball cap she had worn in hopes no one would recognize her, though she wasn't quite sure why it mattered other than she didn't want to see or talk to anyone but Charlie.

"I'm not going to keep doing this to you, Charlie. I promise. I won't make a pest of myself. I shouldn't even be out, but the past six months have seemed ... like years. I've cried all I can cry for a while. I've run out of emotion."

The waitress came. He ordered a Shiner beer on tap, and she ordered a margarita on the rocks. Both were served in large, heavy frosted mugs. Hers had salt around the rim.

"It seems like ages since you staggered into the Methodist Church that Sunday morning. How many years has it been?"

"Not long enough to forget how bad I felt. I thought I was going to die and go to hell right then and there with you giggling by my side."

Comfortable together, they both drank and talked too much about old times, intimate times. That's how Charlie had the nerve to ask and she had the nerve to accept his proposal.

Because Charlie spoke fluent Spanish, one of his clients was an electrical hardware manufacturing company located in Monterrey, Mexico. In four days, he was going to drive down to Monterrey to consult directly with the manufacturer's attorneys about a pending contract to build electrical light switches and outlets. He wouldn't have much free time at first, and he promised he wouldn't make any indecent advances, but if she wanted to come along, he would love the company. It would give her some time away if that's what she needed.

Susan had time to change her mind but the trip excited her, gave her something to look forward to other than black. Like old times she talked to him on the phone the next night, giving him the opportunity to back out if she was going to be in the way.

Because of the impropriety, Susan lied to her family by telling them that she was going to fly out to Santa Fe, New Mexico, and cool off for a few days. It had been hot, and, she explained, she needed a few days to herself.

As planned, Charlie spotted her car in the airport parking lot and pulled up behind it as the sun was beginning to rise over the flatter-than-a-pancake, fertile black dirt farmland that surrounded the Corpus Christi International Airport. He took her suitcase and put it in the trunk of his new '72 blue Buick with the air conditioner set on freezing. Always on full blast, it was as though Texans couldn't get enough of the cool air that blew in from the dashboard like a Blue Norther. Charlie had brought a soft blanket and pillow for the drive that would take them all day.

"Hi."

"Hi."

There was hardly any traffic on the farm roads Charlie took to get to Robstown where they took Highway 44 through Alice to Freer. Susan still looked tired. Her brown eyes had a trace of darkness underneath them.

"Sleeping, Charlie, that's the worst part. They say it's normal, waking up five, six, maybe more times a night. I keep thinking I'll wake up and it will have been a bad dream."

"Breakfast in Laredo," he said as she wedged the pillow in between the door and the seat back and covered herself with the blanket. Looking at her often as she slept, mouth a little open, he felt bad that he had to wake her as they neared the border. The tall, evenly-spaced trees lining the highway of the valley told him they were getting close to the Río Grande, the river separating México from Texas. Known for growing citrus, the valley isn't much of a valley, but that's what it's called.

Charlie ordered "huevos rancheros" for them both at a hotel restaurant he knew from his dove-hunting days with Ivory. After breakfast, crossing the border and clearing customs, they continued south down México Highway 85.

"Charlie," she used his name often when they spoke, and he liked hearing her say it again.

"Charlie, we were normal people getting up each morning, having coffee, eating breakfast, reading the paper, going to work, coming home, having dinner, going to bed. He was a good lover and companion. Did I tell you he was an accountant?

"When I was young, I had visions of a life filled with excitement and glamour. Excitement turned out to be different than I thought. Life is more normal than exciting most of the time. Do you know what I mean, Charlie? Excitement for my husband was getting the company brass to buy a computer. He claims, claimed that is, a whole new world of accounting and data processing is around the corner. We were good for each other. Our interests were different, but we could talk, and we got along.

"I'll bet I haven't even told you what my major was in college, have I?"

"You wanted to teach."

"Art, can you believe it? I was in education until my

senior year. At the time I was seeing a flamboyant drama major. I'll admit *he* was exciting with his wavy black shoulder-length hair. Believe me, a drama major at Southern Methodist University is not your average fraternity-type guy. He was into it, had flair, I'll tell you that. Many a night, we closed a bar called 'The Quiet Man'—though it wasn't too quiet with him talking about poetry and dramatic conflict after we'd all taken psychedelics. We were full of ourselves and ... Art! Rebellion was in the air. Vietnam was everywhere.

"What did you do, Charlie? About the war?"

"Thanks to a tip from Dad, I was able to get into the Army Reserves when they stopped deferments for law school."

"Rational, Charlie, very rational ... and smart.

"Learning to paint and draw was my rebellion. When I told Mom and Dad I was changing majors from Education to Art, they flew up to see if I had flown over the cuckoo's nest. After all the money they'd spent, I don't blame them.

"Let me guess, Charlie, you tried marijuana several times, but stayed away from it because it was illegal?"

"Something like that."

The suspension of the heavy car made her feel as though they were in slow motion, modulating up and down on the uneven Mexican two-lane highway.

"There weren't many law school pot parties, and while I was playing football I barely knew what it was other than trouble."

"Phillip Browning was his name. I keep looking for him in the movies. Anyway, my dad and mom flew up and registered at the Dallas Hyatt Regency. Later that day, their young daughter wearing tie-dye clothes and sandals walked through the lobby and met them in the cocktail lounge. Having smoked half a joint on the way downtown, I ordered a Falstaff long-neck—no glass—and began to tell them how I needed to express my inner self. My dad incredulously pointed out that if I were destined to become a great artist, wouldn't I have painted at least one picture before my senior year of college? What they found when they arrived in Dallas that afternoon was a Texas style, tie-dye, Lone Star, hippie.

"Undaunted, I proceeded to explain to them how the system was manipulated by large corporations that weren't interested in Truth. All they cared about was making tanks and ammunition. Only Art was about *Truth* and the *Soul* of mankind.

"Phillip and I—my parents refused to believe we were living together—we met them for dinner at Cattleman's Steak House. We were Truth personified sitting across from Mom and Dad who, unwittingly, were part of the establishment we so vehemently loathed. Dad, bald as an eagle, was wearing a blue blazer with checkered black and white pants, a red tie and Italian loafers with tassels. Mom had on white high heels, a low-cut cocktail dress, hose, a lot of makeup and perfume.

"Phillip, his hair in a ponytail, was wearing a Nehru-type blue shirt with bell-bottom pants. I was wearing a long cotton dress with a white blouse you could see through—no bra. I had quit wearing contact lenses and was wearing blue-colored granny glasses—'*Lucy In the Sky With Diamonds.*'

"What I put them through. Mother had spent her life crossing her heart with a Maidenform Living Bra, and, here I walk into a Dallas steak house to meet my parents for dinner, and everyone's staring at my tits."

"I wish I'd been there."

Susan smiled as they both noticed a beat-up truck filled with chickens in crates as it passed going the other direction.

"After my senior year, Phillip moved me out of his hippie apartment with Jimi Hendrix on the wall and hash pipes on the floor because, this is how he put it, he needed 'to drink from more than one bottle of wine.'

"On the rebound, not long after Phillip, I met my

husband, former husband that is. Squashed like a bug on a windshield. I shouldn't say it that way, but he was. I'll tell you one thing, a person never imagines her husband is going to be killed by a cabbage truck. You know what? The driver survived. He came to, sat up in the middle of all these cabbages, not knowing what the hell had happened. Now he gets drunk and calls me and cries and tells me how sorry he is. He keeps pointing out how a 10 second nap ruined our lives—10 scheconds, thatchs all. If he had stayed awake just 10 scheconds longer he would have missed, which is true.

"John was a good person, too, a good husband. He really was. Nothing fancy. No frills. Just a decent person who didn't need to drink from every wine bottle he could find. But, I will give Phillip credit for one thing. For the first time in my life, I was doing something that gave me a feeling of accomplishment. I wasn't very good at first, but I've discovered that I have a talent for expression.

"Guess how many paintings I've sold."

"Forty-three."

"Close, five at a student show when I finished my Master's. This dead husband thing has slowed me down.

"Well, I became Mrs. John Richardson, much to my parents' relief. I think they must have offered him a dowry. I told them I wasn't going through with the wedding if they told me one more time how grateful I should be that John came along and saved me from the evil, sinful life I had been living with Phillip. They were overjoyed that John could forgive my wicked ways and make an honest woman out of me.

"Charlie, did you see the movie, *The Graduate*?"

Charlie nodded.

"Did you like it?"

"I thought it was a good movie."

"John thought it was okay, too. I thought it was great ... 'Hello darkness my old friend' — Simon and Garfunkel. Charlie, what do you listen to on the radio when you don't have to listen to me. Country?"

"Not much. Don't forget I'm Ivory and Evett's son. Lots of Mexican. Forties and fifties jazz. I grew up on show tunes."

"I like that....

"How does it feel to be secretly barreling down a Mexican highway with a widow who by any standards of decency should be at home mourning?"

"Despicable."

"Did you love her, your ex? What the hell happened there?"

Susan was wounded, but so was Charlie. His marriage lasting two years had gone embarrassingly poorly, to say the least.

"I suppose I did," Charlie sighed. "But, I usually felt out of place when I was with her Atlanta friends and that should have told me something."

Charlie went on to explain the matrimonial river he felt he had been swept down and the humongous wedding at the humongous country club with the magnolias and champagne. He told her how he felt about Karen on their honeymoon in San Francisco and how he felt about her when he walked in on them and saw the man's pale bare rump going up and down while she looked at him with a startled face that said, "Wait a minute and we'll be finished here."

"Her makeup was still perfect....

"The sad part is, I was still willing to stay with her. The whole concept of a successful marriage and the failure of divorce had me feeling that it was my fault. I felt she went to another man because I wasn't doing my part. A lot of it was ego.

"Real or imagined, it killed me to think of people talking about so-and-so humping my wife behind my back. The whole thing implied that I wasn't man enough to keep my woman satisfied. I begged her not to divorce me. I pleaded with her to try again. I told her I could forgive her, that I would be better.

"Our last night together, the night before I went to basic training—while she was at a meeting, I put on a robe with an ascot for the David Niven look. Thinking I was being funny, I lit candles all over the apartment and iced down a bottle of champagne, the kind we had had at our wedding.

"When she got home for our big farewell night together, she came through the door, looked around and said, 'Charlie, what is going on? Jesus Christ, Charlie, you really *don't* understand, do you?' Then she turned, went to the bedroom and closed the door. I couldn't figure out how she had come to dislike me the way she did. I had no idea what I had done.

"Then, if you can believe this, after being totally humiliated, I stood in line at the pay phone outside the Army barracks to call her and asked her to start over. She was right when she said I didn't understand."

"Oh, Charlie ...." Susan put her bare feet on his thigh ... on and on the conversation went until they reached the outskirts of Monterrey and, unfolding the city map, began navigating their way downtown to El Hotel Presidente.

It was late by the time they finished dinner at the restaurant in the grandiose lobby filled with greenery.

"Charlie, thank you for letting me tag along. Lie

down on the bed and let me rub your back. You must be exhausted."

In silence, they had said all they could for one day, she worked the muscles on his shoulders and neck, the ones that felt tight from the drive.

The next morning, Susan awoke to a different world. Even the telephones were different. When she knocked and then entered his room, the sun was up and Charlie was gone. She took her time showering and had breakfast in a solarium attended by waiters in starched white shirts before going to the pool with her book.

Sitting in the lounge chair beside the manicured garden surrounding the pool, she was immediately aware of the absence of piteous notoriety. In Corpus she felt that everywhere she went people were staring at her.

"That's the girl whose husband was killed several months ago outside of Victoria. Hit by a cabbage truck."

Suddenly, in Mexico, she was an anonymous person who wasn't supposed to be sad all the time. She could smile her genuine smile. She was just another tourist sitting by the swimming pool reading a paperback.

After eating an enchilada dinner alone in the lobby, Susan was on the edge of sleep when Charlie quietly opened the door and whispered into her dark room, "Are you asleep?"

"How'd it go?"

"Okay, I'll tell you all about it at breakfast. We're invited to a party tomorrow night."

Exhausted, he caught himself before, "Love you," slipped out.

The next day, after breakfast, while Charlie was going over the final drafts of the contract written in both Spanish and English, Susan went shopping for an appropriate dress at an upscale boutique on the square. She wasn't fluent in Spanish but she knew enough to buy a dress.

When packing for the trip, she hadn't even thought about going to a festive occasion, so it was a morning of symbolic renewal. At least that is how she thought of it as she tried things on.

Later, feeling alive and pretty, she showered, put on her makeup and slipped the new dress over her head before putting on a faint touch of perfume and new high heels. Then she knocked on Charlie's door to find him in a pair of slacks, sports shirt and light sports jacket.

As they went down the elevator she asked, "Who do these people think I am? I'm honestly nervous. Will they speak any English?"

Charlie put his hands on her waist, she smiled and he gave her a quick kiss on the lips. She looked great.

"There will be a lot of food, a lot of drinks and a lot of laughter because it's a signed deal. And, I'm very glad you're here," he said as the elevator door of the hotel opened into the lobby and she put her arm through his as they walked to the foyer and got into the shiny black Mercedes that had been sent for them.

"So, I'm your harlot?"

After feeling very old for six months, Susan was smiling even though it felt surreal to be a grieving widow standing next to this man, Charlie Jones, in Mexico, acting almost like newlyweds among strangers speaking mostly Spanish.

The house they went to was huge with an extravagant patio inside the walled hacienda. Waiters were everywhere with refreshments. When they sat down in the large dining room, they were asked if they preferred filet mignon or Maine lobster. The various wines were superb as each course was served, and Charlie was a dear as he introduced her.

After dinner, the men edged their way to the tiled patio to smoke Cuban cigars and have brandy while the women stayed in the dining room, refreshing themselves in the powder room—all quite provincial and charmingly foreign.

Soon afterwards, thanking the hosts and saying

their goodbyes, Charlie had the driver take them back to El Presidente where he had a chilled bottle of Chardonnay sent to his room.

They were both laughing when they got out of the elevator, but were silent as they walked down the hall to unlock the door with a heavy brass key. Inside, they closed the door, put their arms around each other and kissed.

"Charlie," she pulled back and looked right into his eyes, "I think you'd better make love to me. I'm ready to see you again."

Chapter VII

Getting to Know You

THERE was a thin stream of light coming into the hotel room where the curtains didn't quite meet at the center. Charlie, facing Susan's back, squinted at the brightness as he propped his head up on his hand and looked at her hair and the way it fell around her neck. He had never seen anything so perfect.

After a while, he slowly, and as quietly as he could, slipped from underneath the covers and went into the bathroom. Looking at himself in the mirror he didn't look like the type of person who would repeatedly take advantage of a recently widowed woman. What an ugly word—"widow." Maybe it wasn't the word, maybe it was the image it conjured up. How was this going to play out? The mirror on the wall reflected the image of a man shaving and hoping.

As he came out of the shower, through the open door he could hear the shower in the adjoining room. Not sure what to do, he took the towel from around his waist and put on some boxer shorts before opening the first layer of curtains.

The Hotel Presidente was doing a good job of keeping the Monterrey heat from their small part of its world. Each room, he thought, well maybe not each room, but several rooms he guessed were the host of human drama. "Human drama," Charlie's plot had, in a very short period of time, thickened considerably.

In the shower in her own room, Susan mechanically washed her hair and applied conditioner the way she always did before she first put her right then her left leg on the shower wall to shave them. With a towel wrapped around her body and another one around her hair, she walked through the common doors connecting the rooms to find Charlie sitting on the bed in his underwear.

"Oh, Charlie, what in the world have we done now?"

"Susan, Susan, Susan, I wish I knew what to say. It's easy for me to say how life goes on, but I'm not the one whose husband is all of a sudden gone. I'm sure you thought you were going to grow old together, have children and worry about them growing up—all of that with him."

They were hugging each other when he told her that he loved her, which made her hug him even harder and cry even more.

"Look, let's go easy. Dry your eyes, and let's go downstairs for breakfast. I have an idea you can think about while I finish up business this afternoon. I need about two or three, maybe four hours, and I'm free."

Susan was muscular in a woman's way, not big, but deceivingly solid and strong. Her breasts, which were paler than the rest of her from wearing a bikini top, had Charlie going again. His underwear looked like a teepee as he attempted to look over the paperwork in front of him while glancing back at her. There was no way to talk over the noise of the hair dryer, and there was no way he could comprehend the words he was trying to read. The smell of the heating element burning tiny atmospheric particles of dust and the mingling of drying hair with the fragrance of her bath soap was luxuriously intimate. He hoped with all his heart it was something he would smell for the rest of his life.

"Come on Charlie, I want you, too," Susan said

when she came out of her trance and looked at Charlie in a condition reminiscent of that fateful Sunday at the First Methodist Church. "It isn't anything we haven't done before." Her teeth were remarkably even. He remembered her braces.

It was Friday. Charlie's idea was to wrap things up in Monterrey and take a flight to Mexico City the next day. They could fly back to Monterrey on Sunday and then drive to Corpus in time for him to get to the office on Tuesday.

The next morning, looking at the colorful houses through the window during their descent, the piston-driven Convair AeroMéxico airplane that rattled with a devil-may-care attitude touched down on the runway and taxied to the tarmac.

In Mexico City, they took the peso taxis up and down the Paseo, visited the palace at Chapultepec, laughed and touched at the Villa Fontana surrounded by violins and dueling grand pianos, had a nightcap at the top of the Latin American Tower overlooking the lights of the city—and made love in the Gran Hotel before they caught a plane that rattled them back to Monterrey.

Susan was tired, but she needed to talk as they drove north toward Nuevo Laredo. The sky had gone from pink to dark blue as the Buick's headlights began to illuminate the road in front of them.

"We looked silly at the Villa Fontana, you know that, Charlie, don't you? I mean no one really takes a girl to hear violins and puts his hand on her thigh under the table. Must be your Latin blood. Tell me more about your parents."

"You should have seen them at the Atlanta Country Club wedding. Dad *does* play the piano and sell hardware. Mom *is* a Latina Hollywood actress from California, and I *am* a half-breed."

Charlie told her a few amusing, incorrigible Ivory and enchanted Evett stories. "I've thought about it a lot, who Dad is, I mean. I've always thought he was slightly crazy, but you know, he just does things the way he wants to do them and honestly doesn't give a flip what anyone thinks. God, he can get on my nerves.

"A lot of it has to do with his hand, losing it or part of it. He was a serious piano player when he met Mom, before the war, supposedly one of the best. According to Mom, it was his ability to shade notes, improvise and arrange that set him apart from the others, until he lost his fingers. He's figured out how to play with his glove contraption, but the injury killed their plans. They really didn't want to come back to Corpus Christi. Bitter pills to swallow.

"This is what the sign said that he put over the counter at the hardware store:

WARNING!
DO NOT MAKE ME MAD
I'M ALMOST OUT OF HAND AS IT IS

Charlie told her about his dad's glove innovation and how well he was able to keep a bass line going with it.

"And Mom, I'll show you her films—amazingly talented."

In silence, lost in their own thoughts, they continued silently down the highway for a while.

"Charlie, would you marry me?

"Charlie, I think I know your heart and what kind of person you are, but I don't know a lot of your details, what you do for fun these days, what makes you mad, what's your favorite color. You'll probably watch football on Sunday. I wonder if we'll get along.

"Will you, Charlie?"

Pulling off on the highway shoulder and stopping, "This is what I was hoping for."

As the world spun and the sun dropped behind the desert sand, "Last night I said what I guess I would call a prayer—with my knees touching the backside of your legs.

John has to understand. Oh, I don't really think he's up on some cloud looking down on us. If I were up there, I'd want this for him. Charlie, I need you, and I want you. I hope we'll be good to each other. Look both ways before crossing the street, will you Charlie?" She was frowning.

On the real-life side of their own human drama, she knew they were going to have to plan an explanation of how they got to know each other so soon, so well, and how she happened to fall in love so quickly after her terrible loss. Susan couldn't possibly rush in and tell her mother and father that she had run off to México, fallen in love with an old friend that she had experimentally fucked in high school in her own bedroom no less, and now wanted to marry. On the other hand, neither Charlie nor Susan, especially Susan, could see waiting too long because things can happen. Things can go bad.

Fantasizing about Charlie while she was by the pool at the Hotel Presidente, she had come up with a make-believe plan. She'd inherited some money, quite a bit of money from her late husband's company life insurance plan and the trucking firm's liability insurance settlement.

It would only be natural for her to go to her old friend, now attorney-at-law Charlie Jones, for professional legal and financial advice. They would accidentally fall in love, which would shock everyone, and get married too soon, which would shock everyone. For sure, tongues were going to be wagging in old C.C. by the seaside, sparkling city by the sea, and only Susan and Charlie could truly understand.

"Charlie, we've got to do what is right for us. I can only do so much for appearance's sake with our lives hanging in the balance."

She stuck to her guns as she was inclined. Her parents had survived Susan's wild college days with Phillip, then the death of their daughter's new husband, their first son-in-law. Somehow, they would ride this out.

Where to have the wedding was the next problem. Susan and her parents knew that having a church wedding so soon would be in very poor taste. Likewise, as close as Susan's parents had become with her former husband's parents, they felt uncomfortable having the wedding in their home. So, it was decided, with a little help from Evett, that they would have a civil ceremony at Charlie's parent's home.

To placate Susan's mother's concerns, the wedding was going to be a low-key affair in light of the fact that John Richardson had not been dead a full year. A year was the minimum amount of time Susan should have waited just to date. Naturally, Susan's side of the family was hyper-apprehensive and worried about whether their daughter was rushing into something too soon.

On the other side of the fence, Ivory and Evett were delighted. They'd liked her since grade school.

In Corpus Christi, there were several tiers of social hierarchy. At the top were old families with old money. Just beneath them on the social ladder were new families with new money—Susan's parents. One rung lower were the people struggling to break into the Country Club society. Below them were, well, the others.

Somewhere in their midst were the people in Ivory and Evett's circle of friends—teachers, musicians, furniture makers, writers, Little Theater actors and the like.

Ivory's ragtime version of "Here Comes the Bride" set the tone for the ceremony. The custom glove he used for his piano playing had become much more sophisticated since he discovered the golf glove. Made of thin, soft leather it was designed to fit the left hand snugly. There were even perforations to keep the hand cool.

Ivory had become so enamored with the golf glove he wore while he worked at the lumberyard. With it, there was no maimed flesh to stare at. The irony—that he looked like a golfer—was not lost on Ivory who was doubly delighted that he could buy the left glove, without having to buy a pair of gloves. Not only that, golf gloves came in a variety of colors. If Ivory wore a blue shirt, he'd wear a blue matching glove. It tickled him immensely.

Evett looked splendid in an exquisite dress she picked out for the occasion. Ivory looked rather dapper himself.

After the wedding cake had been cut and served, they all drank a heartfelt toast to the bride and groom.

Chapter VIII

The Big Time

HAL had been gone for 10 days, calling in only three times to see how she and the kids were doing. There were two now. Over the phone, he sounded vague about what was going on and a little punchy from lack of sleep. Red was tired and up to her ears in redheaded kids who were alternately nice to each other or at each other's throats. She often felt she should be wearing a referee's shirt, because each of the kids knew exactly how to push the other one's button.

"I'll share with you, okay?"

"No, I'll share with you."

"I said I'd share with you first. I got first dibs on

sharing."

They could argue about anything.

The trailer was too small. She needed Hal around much more than he had been.

"Daddy!" they both yelled as his El Camino left a trail of dust on the dirt road leading to the small fenced-in yard that kept the cows away from the front porch. He swung the kids around and then gave Red a big hug. His unshaven face felt like sandpaper as it scraped her cheek.

"It ain't Corpus Christi, but it ain't Cuero either," Hal said excitedly, hinting at big changes to come.

He couldn't get the grin off his face no matter how aggravated Red was, and her aggravation quickly turned to astonishment when she learned how suddenly they had become wealthy, literally, overnight. The rig Hal had begged and borrowed to buy was badly in need of a major overhaul. All three of the mammoth diesels were losing compression and burning oil. On the third, and perhaps final shot for Harlequin Oil, he'd taken a big chance. It was a hunch. On a small farm located not far from Alice, Texas, Hal hit a big one.

Alone in the trailer bedroom with about a foot on either side of the mattress, after some serious lovemaking, they finally had a chance to talk about their future.

"Hal, I can't pack up and leave tomorrow. You

know we need a *place* to move *to*. I can pack what we've got, but Hal where are we going? I've got to say goodbye to this town that has been my home for my whole life."

Red had wanted to leave for so long, yet it was sad to think she was going to move away from the Dairy Queen and the pharmacy down the street from Hap's Diner.

"Red, we're only going to Robstown, 145 miles from here. Three hours max in your new car. You can drive here whenever you want."

"Hal, I want one of those Ford Fairlane Convertibles, a red one with white trim. You'd better not be pulling my leg about that well. I *will* look good with the top down."

"You *always* look good with the top down."

Now, Robstown may not sound like much more than Cuero, and in a lot of ways it wasn't. But, located in between Corpus Christi and Kingsville, Hal was going to try to get in on the drilling being done at the King Ranch, which was over a million acres big and short on cash. The King family's tastes had become more and more refined, and breeding their own cattle had been expensive.

The other cause for the cash squeeze was the fact that the family had grown. Children married and had children, so there were a lot of dependents who, in complicated ways, owned a share of the King Ranch. This being Texas, there was a lot of intrigue and whiskey as Hal maneuvered for a piece of the action.

Robstown, with a three-block downtown, was strategically the logical place to locate Harlequin Oil and Gas. It was close enough to Kingsville, yet only 30 minutes from the big city, Corpus Christi, with an airport, a train station and a major seaport. With cash in the bank, he was negotiating to purchase a new rig and several prospective drilling rights. Hal figured there had to be oil under the King family's million acres. With Harlequin luck he'd find some of it.

Red and Hal loaded their cars and drove to their new home, a two-story, wood-frame house with a wrap-around porch that Red had found on the outskirts of town. Tellingly, they were able to stuff the kids and all their possessions into the two cars and make the move in one trip.

After having the house painted inside and out, they went to Sears and Roebuck to buy all new appliances and furniture — "Ranch Style." Red knew Sears.

At first, they had gone to a swanky furniture store in Corpus where Red felt she could maybe get used to the modern, futuristic sofas, divans, and chairs that were as much a part of the 1950's "in" style as were the spaceship-tailfins on new cars. Much to Hal's relief, she chose to sit on Sear's "Ranch Style" couches and put their drinks on a "Ranch Style" coffee table. They bought the entire five-piece ensemble, including a "Ranch Style" television cabinet.

Soon after they settled into the new home and enrolled the kids in the Robstown public school system, a wonderful thing happened to Red. She, by chance, discovered the Corpus Christi Public Library. It was nothing out of the ordinary for a town the size of Corpus, but it was a grand revelation to her. Within its quiet confines, there were so many books about everything on heaven and earth, it made the hair on her arms stand on end.

There was a whole section of cookbooks that included recipes on how to prepare fish. Until the move, Red had never eaten seafood other than canned shrimp. The first time she had them at Hap's Diner in Cuero, they were served on the rim of a glass Jell-O bowl filled with ketchup. What was even more pitiful, she thought it was some kind of drink before it was brought to the table. Curiosity's why she'd ordered it in the first place.

Seeing the books on every subject imaginable was, she thought laughing to herself, like discovering the tomb of Zorba if there even was a tomb of Zorba.

The other wonderful thing about their Robstown life was that Hal came home for dinner most nights. With his recent good fortune, Hal went from being a roughneck who owned a run-down rig to a small oil company entrepreneur with two rigs—from laborer to deal maker. Harlequin Oil and Gas was a good name, because it stuck in people's minds. If asked, Hal would explain how his wife loved to read Harlequin novels and about his promise to her if his well came in.

Driving back and forth from Corpus Christi in her new red convertible, Red was fast becoming redneck literate. As soon as she got the kids off to school, she cleaned up the house in a flurry so she could get into her latest stack of books.

The discovery was so profound, Red pushed both kids well beyond the Robstown Public School System's capabilities. Both would be the first in their combined families to go to college.

Surprising himself, Hal came upon a discovery of his own. Waiting for some heavy equipment to be unloaded from a freighter, he walked the two T-heads and the one L-head that extended from downtown into Corpus Christi Bay. Sheltered by a breakwater made of granite boulders, were slips for small boats like the *Antonia K* and the *Lydia Pinkum*. What kind of person would name a boat the *Lydia Pinkum*? Who lived on the *Antonia K*? For Hal, it was as though he was walking into the Sunday funny papers, up and down the comic strips. They were the funniest little things he had ever seen. Boats to Hal had been warships, freighters and pirate ships. In Cuero, he was only vaguely aware of fishing boats from pictures.

> Shrimp boats are a coming
> There's dancing tonight
> Shrimp boats are a coming
> Their sails are in sight

The two T-heads, the L-head and the breakwater were constructed during the Great Depression of the 1930's as a WPA (Works Progress Administration) project whose goal was to pump money into the economy with "make work" projects. Large cement piers and the cement steps that went down 30 feet from Ocean Drive to the water had become part of Corpus Christi's personality. This is where people would come to square dance on Saturday night to a live band or watch the Fourth of July fireworks that were shot from a barge out in the bay.

Ocean Drive "Downtown" was divided by a wide grass median fringed with palm trees. On Sundays, these medians were football fields for local boys playing tackle without shirts, shoes or helmets. Shrimp could be bought on the L-head (25 cents a pound for jumbos) where there were two free ramps for launching boats from trailers.

Without a doubt, Hal's favorite boat was the *Gulf Clipper*. It was a 60-foot, double-decked excursion boat with a wooden hull. On the first deck, there were life rafts, red life preservers and places to sit with cushions. On the upper deck, behind the wheelhouse, was a large, varnished wood dance floor. But, it wasn't flat. It had a curve from stem to stern. At the same time, athwartship, from port to starboard, there was a convex curve to keep water from sitting and rotting the shiny decks.

One night, for the hell of it, he talked Red into taking the evening cruise. The smell of the boat and the sea were senses they had never encountered. Just aft of the wheelhouse on the upper deck, a trio with congas and a guitar played music while people tried to dance on the rocking, rolling, curving decks. Looking up at the stars while the ship's engine rumbled quietly, Hal could sense the immensity.

As it came to pass, about once a month, Hal got behind the wheel of the red convertible, and drove Red to Corpus and the T-head for a night of stars and water. A secret getaway.

She was almost as fascinated with the *Gulf Clipper* as Hal. While the conga players played and the guitar player swayed, amplified through a two-foot square Fender amplifier, Hal and Red would nose around the boat. The captain didn't mind if they stood with him in the dark wheelhouse, illuminated by a few instruments and a large brass compass. The wheelhouse was the only part of the boat that wasn't lit up because the captain had to see the lights of the channel markers in the shallow bay.

Going out, the lights of Corpus got smaller and smaller. Naturally, the reverse was true when they were coming back to the breakwater and the dock. With his arms around Red, sitting on the cushioned seats that were part of the upper deck railing—surrounded by lovers necking and dancers dancing—Hal could put aside life's everyday problems and just be alone with Red, who continuously fascinated him. She knew something about everything.

He never would have seen Manhattan, or gone to see the play, *Evita*, had it not been for Red's insatiable inquisitiveness. He never would have taken a month off to drive through parts of Europe, nor would he have seen Adam and Eve upside down in California.

On the *Gulf Clipper* they laughed about how they felt like strangers on earth peeking in on other people's lives. Alien observers sent down from Cuero and Goliad to see what in the world was going on. It was on the *Gulf Clipper* that Hal returned to the railing with a couple of beers, ice flakes dripping off the bottles, to find tears running down Red's cheeks because she loved him so much.

Chapter IX

The Show

CHARLIE and Susan's first years were simply too good to be true. They pinched one another to remind themselves they were once again happily among the living.

She applied for and was hired as an assistant professor in the art department at Del Mar Junior College, teaching two classes—a job she was thrilled with.

"Rome wasn't built in a day," she was prone to say as she encouraged her students to paint the same subject over and over to improve their skills. An artist could read about color and look at the way other artists handled their subject, but there was no substitute for the brush or palette knife in their own hands.

Susan drove a seven-year-old station wagon because she liked to work on her canvases both at school and at home in her studio. She liked her old car that smelled like oil paint. If they needed to go anywhere, they could go in Charlie's 1974 very chic Buick Riviera.

Quietly, alone, she had been working on a series of paintings that caused their first *major* argument. He could not understand her choice of subject matter and knew it was going to cause nothing but trouble.

"I don't have any idea why you would do such a thing. All you are going to do is upset people while they're trying to heal. Do your mom and dad know what you're doing? No, I didn't think so. You are going to cause a major uproar and hurt a lot of feelings. Don't you feel some responsibility to John's memory? I don't know if I want my wife showing things like that. Okay, okay. I know I don't own you, but what you do reflects on me. I simply can't believe it. Nudes—why couldn't you just paint nudes, male nudes—anything but what you're doing here?"

"Charlie, I lived with this day and night for a long time. It haunts me. It happened. It's life, Charlie. We don't all grow old and die in our sleep. Anyway, I got the idea from a country song. I thought you'd like that. All I've done is paint a raw part of my life. Everybody knows what happened, anyhow."

"But Susan it's sick, it's not healthy. It's like you're trying to be the weird artist type."

"Good, real good, Charlie, we should all be like you —conforming lawyers who defend only innocent people, do the right thing all of the time and live happily forever and ever after."

Charlie was beside himself as Susan sang, her voice quivering with emotion, the song that had been part of her inspiration:

Blood on the saddle
Blood on the ground
A great big puddle of blood all around
A cowboy lay in it
All covered with gore
He'll never ride bucking broncos no more
Oh, pity the cowboy
All bloody and red
A bronco fell on him and crushed in his head

Hanging on the walls of the South Bluff Gallery on opening night were a series of paintings, all done on different sized canvases. The first one was of a little girl skipping rope in the backyard. The next one had a girl wearing a cap and gown, her parents standing on either side of her, beaming with pride. The third painting was of a bride and groom cutting their wedding cake.

The first paintings in the series were not realistic. They looked as though they were out of focus. They were gauzy with a lot of color. The definition of the paintings became more and more clear as the series progressed. The fourth painting showed a field where crops were being planted. In the background was a large thundercloud with rain coming down underneath the cumulus buildup. The sun was still shining on the couple who were doing the planting—earth, sun, crops, mankind and rain.

The fifth painting was of a truck filled with cabbage speeding along the highway. Up ahead was a car on the side of the road. A man was changing a tire. The Ford truck was red, with transparent sides, so the person looking at the painting could see what the truck was carrying.

The final painting, the only one in perfect focus, was the largest. On a five-by-five-foot canvas was a large cabbage. The colors were brilliant and the cabbage was painted sensually with droplets of water on the veins of the shiny leaves. Life and death—the huge cabbage was sitting in a pool of blood.

"'Blood on the Cabbage'—that's the name of the series, Charlie."

"Jesus Christ, Susan, how could you do this? Why?"

"I don't know who you thought you were marrying, Charlie Jones. It is becoming clear that you wanted a nice little wife who knows her place. A pretty little thing who paints pictures of flowers and clowns. Thanks a lot, Charlie. I find the image of who you want me to be sickening. Do you know what makes me the maddest, Charlie? You don't take what I do seriously. You think what you do is more important, and the wonderful opinion you have of yourself is reinforced by the fact that you make a lot more money than I do. Look, go handle your lawsuits and leave me alone."

"Oh, so now I'm an immoral attorney because I don't like what you are painting. Come on Susan, 'Blood on the Cabbage'??"

It was an ugly night.

Understandably, Susan's parents felt like they had been hit by too many bean balls. They would have talked very ungraciously about the antics of this person had she been someone else's daughter. Everything was black and white and then along came color.

At the opening with Pinot Grigio in their wine glasses, Mr. and Mrs. Duncan felt terribly out of place. Bewildered, in his gray suit beside his wife dressed in her cocktail attire, they tried to take it all in and absorb what people were saying about their daughter's work despite the fact that they wouldn't take traffic directions from the type of people who were complimentary.

The society writer for the cultural page of the *Corpus Christi Caller-Times* diplomatically described the paintings as "wonderful renderings of childhood dreams and adult realities."

The opening, Susan had to admit, was a disaster. For those who came, it was uncomfortable. How do you compliment the artist whose paintings depict a terrible personal tragedy when the terrible personal tragedy was hers?

Susan would survive. So would Charlie, though it was every bit as awkward as he imagined it would be.

In the locker room at the country club, he took the kidding somewhat good-naturedly. "You've got your hands full with that little filly, don't you?"

Charlie was trying hard to learn the game of golf. Having been denied a country club childhood he was trying to catch up, and it was a humbling experience. Ex-jock, strong as a bull, Charlie couldn't hit the ball half as far as the golf pro who had a gimp leg. But, Charlie approached golf as he had everything else, with perseverance and determination.

Susan's father, Brad, who was more on Charlie's wavelength than he was his own daughter's, was the first to invite him to play a round. Charlie soon became a member of their regular Saturday golf bunch.

And as it so happened, after a game of golf, Charlie invited Susan's parents, along with Ivory and Evett, to their house to hear the good news and celebrate.

Susan was pregnant.

As thrilled as they were, Susan's dad inwardly winced when he thought about what Ivory, with his arm around Evett, had said to him as they shook hands. "Brad, this little baby's going to have our genes. Congratulations to us!!" he said, as he sat down at the piano and started playing every song he knew that had the word "baby" in it. The conversations continued as Ivory did what he liked to do. He could easily carry on a conversation and play the piano at the same time.

> Baby face
> You've got the cutest little baby face
> I'm in heaven
> When I feel your warm embrace

Lamaze and natural childbirth were "in," and drugs were "out" in 1975 when Jeffrey was born. Charlie knew from his law practice that 30% maybe 40% of those attending the classes would eventually divorce—probably five out of the 12 in attendance. But, that would be further down the road. The men showed genuine concern and affection for the women who, according to nature's plan, were going to experience substantially more of the miracle of birth than their spouses.

When the actual moment came for Charlie and Susan, the only real pain Charlie felt was from the ring on his finger as Susan gripped his hand like a vise.

Unable to go to sleep after their son's debut, they drank a bottle of wine together in the hospital room as tiny little Jeffrey suckled up to his mama just as Mother Nature intended.

They were simple over Jeffrey—the first smiles, the finger holding, the first steps. At age three Jeffrey was as adorable as a child could be. Out of diapers, he was proud of pooping in the toilet. New words and mispronunciations were all a part of it. The "leming room" was the living room. Shoes were "foosh."

"Oh-tay."

First there was soccer. Run and kick; kick and run. Susan couldn't believe how enthusiastic Charlie was during the games. Obviously, it had come from his days as a football player.

Watching Jeffrey grow and learn were wonderfully happy times. So innocent, it was hard to believe he would grow up so soon, get pimples and start growing hair on his legs.

Chapter X

A House on the Hill

MR. AND MRS. C. JONES
3140 Ocean Drive
Corpus Christi, Texas

"Charlie, you say we can afford it. You want it badly, so I say let's do it."

Charles G. Jones, Esq., now had two Latino attorneys working with him in adjacent offices as his law practice had become highly successful in negotiating international business contracts involving México and several other Latin American countries. Charlie had become a big deal in this specialized niche.

"It will be sad leaving this little place."

But, leave it they did. They closed on the new house and began moving out of their first and only home. The pool was going to be good for Jeffrey and his friends on those summer afternoons when swimming was the only thing 11-year-olds weren't tired of doing. He could jump in after baseball practice and cool down.

Susan would have some great places to put up her easel. For Charlie, it was a dream come true. It was the crown jewel of his professional success. He, Charlie Jones, had worked hard and now could afford to live in a house that was not only a symbol, it was something he and his family could enjoy together. It was a measure of his achievements.

Charlie, Susan, and Jeff pulled into the circular brick drive the day after the movers had completed removing the last of the previous owner's furniture. Even Jeffrey was impressed.

In the living room was the only piece of furniture left behind. Majestically sitting on the flawlessly white carpet was Ivory's housewarming present—a black Steinway B grand piano. He liked Steinways.

Charlie, Susan and then Jeffrey, in single file, went from room to room, peeking inside the closets and doors that were now theirs. The breakfast room, next to the kitchen, had an outdoor patio with a fountain. The dining room was covered with the same flawless white carpet that was in the living room. As they walked through, they thought they heard the phone ring and tried to locate it. It rang again which was baffling because the phone hadn't even been installed yet.

The "garden room" was large enough to have two trees growing toward the skylight of the 24-foot-high ceiling. Copper sheathing covered the wall above the oversized fireplace. The floors were Mexican terracotta, stained and waxed to a gloss. They felt small looking around the cavernous, empty room.

To the left of the entranceway, down the hall, were three bedrooms, each overlooking Corpus Christi Bay and the swimming pool. The carpets in the bedrooms, living room and dining room were bordered with black or light tan Italian marble depending on their location.

Looking out at the bay, they could see two men who were fishing in waders about 100 yards from their seawall. As you faced 3140 Ocean Drive from the street, there was a ravine between the Jones' and their neighbors to the right. Fresh water from a small stream that had been routed underground by developers fed into the ocean, making it one of the best fishing spots along that part of the bay's coast.

The fishermen would park on the other side of

Ocean Drive, walk across the street, down the gulch and out into the shallows. Usually they caught trout, but occasionally they would catch a big red fish.

Ivory had already ordered a new pair of waders and a floating tackle box.

Susan's studio was going to be in the garden room. On that, she insisted. Charlie wanted her to convert the garage, but good luck with that. It was her house, too, and if she wanted to make a mess in one of the corners, goody two-shoes was just going to have to get used to it. Charlie argued that the paint smell and the inevitable mess she produced would detract from the beauty of the room and the decor.

"Tough luck, big boy. If I can't enjoy it, then I'm moving back to the old place, and you can sleep alone in your mansion on the hill." No way in hell was she going to be stuck in the garage.

Grudgingly, Charlie had a raised plywood floor covered with teak parquet built for Susan's corner of the world. The wood would be easier on her feet and it would protect the tile floor from oil paint. If company was coming, they could put up a screen to hide her mess.

When the moving and decorating was mostly complete, Charlie and Susan organized an elaborate housewarming party with a bartender and waitress from the country club and two cooks from Mac's, where Susan and Charlie had met for the first time after John's death. It was quite an affair with music by Ivory's trio—Evett on bass and a drummer.

Afterwards, when the guests had gone home, the biggest thing bothering Susan was the fact that the house and the trappings meant she was rich. She feared her friends who had been comfortable in the old house were going to feel out of place in the new digs. Susan tended to dress down, while her parents and Charlie dressed up.

Susan liked her shitty station wagon and the group of people trying to make ends meet that she interacted with daily. Now people were going to say, "Well, she doesn't have to worry about money; she's married to a hotshot lawyer. She can afford to sit around all day and paint pictures."

She tried to talk to Charlie about how she felt.

"You live in a home people dream of living in. Your friends are just envious," Charlie explained.

"That's not what I'm talking about, Charlie. There is something about making ends meet with your talent that creates a bond."

"Susan, that's what we've done. Our talent is what is making the mortgage payments."

"Charlie, it's as though we aren't common people

anymore."

"I don't want to be a common person."

"I don't mean common like common, Charlie, or average. I guess I mean we aren't regular Joes anymore. In the other house, we were like so many other people. Some houses were better than others, and some had a pool, but we were all pretty much the same. Our lots were about the same size. Anyone from the houses like our old one is going to come in here and think they are in the Taj Mahal. This place is seriously intimidating. I like our old friends. I don't want to lose them … Charlie, I don't know who our neighbors are. No one seems to be home in the house next to us, and the one on the other side of the gully is so far away, the people look small walking around on the lawn, which you have to admit is extremely large. I don't know if they could hear me if I yelled at them."

"I think I am starting to get it. You think that what I make is more than I should? Is that what you're saying—that we don't deserve this, and we should be like everyone else? I don't understand why you aren't proud of me and happy we can live like this. Instead, you're telling me you're ashamed?"

"Oh, Charlie, I am proud of you, maybe it's guilt I'm feeling."

"Isn't this great. Now you want to move back to our

old house so you can be like everyone else. You're a fraud, pretending to be a struggling artist when you have a fat bank account to back you up.

"I mean, you artist types are too much. You want to earn from your *Art*, yet you paint something like 'Blood on the Cabbage,' which no one was going to buy. All you did was shock people who genuinely miss a man you happened to be married to who was unlucky enough to be hit by a fucking cabbage truck.

"Meanwhile, I am the evil capitalist pig that you pseudo-hippies love to hate. This grand vision you have of yourself struggling against the world and people like me is horseshit, and don't even mention Ivory and Evett. I don't want to hear about my saintly nut of a mother and father who've got quite a stash in the bank themselves. He's so busy being the great common man he doesn't spend any of it."

"Charlie, calm down. You're right. I'm not trying to hurt your feelings. I'm just trying to talk to you. And, remember, would you Charlie, the luck you had with your ex who had puffy nipples and perfect makeup." Charlie knew it was a mistake to have told Susan about the puffy nipples.

"Oh, by the way, Charlie, you know the phone ring we keep hearing when there's no one on the line? I found it, the ring that is."

"What was it?"

"If you look closely, there is a slight bump in the carpet next to the place at the head of the table in the dining room." Charlie had bought a black, perfectly lacquered table with gold leaf ivy carved in the legs. Seating eight, the chairs were soft, light brown leather bordered with a matching black lacquered wood frame.

"Come here, Charlie." They left the kitchen and went to the dining room. Located at the head of the table, Susan stepped on an almost imperceptible bump on the rug. In the kitchen, a bell rang.

"This your Royal Highness, is how the Master calls the kitchen help. Just buzz me when you want me, honey, and I'll come a-runnin'."

Charlie couldn't keep the smile from his face no matter how hard he tried.

Chapter XI

You Did What?

THOUGH it wasn't easy, Susan slowly adjusted to the new house, in large part, due to her corner of the world, which she maintained carelessly in the ways of a painter. On her plywood platform along with one of the living room chairs and the couch from the old house, her area turned out to be where she and her friends most often congregated—much to Charlie's chagrin. To him, her studio looked like the stage at the Community Theater except that this ragged, paint-splotched work area was *in the middle of their home.*

"No Charlie, I don't have a clue as to how the paint got on the wall. I'll see if it comes off with turpentine, okay?"

The light from the skylight over her easel was fantastic, no matter what time of day it was. After dark, two of the light switches with dimmers could be turned up. Although she rarely worked at night, she liked to look over what she had done that day, and she enjoyed socializing in her space.

Compared to the size of the room, hers was a small area, but it commanded attention. She used a Craftsman tool box on rollers, the kind professional mechanics use, to store tubes of paint, brushes and palette knives. Naturally, even more so than the walls, it was covered with splotches of color. Charlie diplomatically offered to buy her a new one with the implied agreement that she would keep it cleaner.

"How could I concentrate on what I am doing if I have to constantly clean a new tool box?"

He said he was just trying to make things nice for her.

With its back to the room, the old sofa faced a window where Susan could see the waves crash into the cement seawall at the bottom of the gently sloping bluff. When the wind blew hard, as it often did, sheets of spray—10, sometimes 15 feet high—shot into the air.

In summer, the garden room made her feel as

though she was outside minus the wind and the heat. During winter months, the mesquite-fueled fire made the room cozy despite its size.

Susan's skill as an artist had improved substantially over the years and her paintings sold well. But, her biggest thrill artistically and spiritually came when she was commissioned to do a large 20-by-60-foot mosaic tile mural for the new Parkdale State Bank building. Her interest in mosaic had been piqued by a 1950's mural done by Mary Sloan, which covered the front of the auditorium on the Del Mar College campus. Daily she had passed this larger-than-life depiction of shrimp boats with flowing nets and rust-stained hulls.

At first, feeling overwhelmed by the enormity of the task, she contacted Mrs. Sloan, who still resided in Corpus. Through friends, she learned that it had been completed not long before the tragic death of Mrs. Sloan's son, Walter, who died at age 12 from bone cancer. Though Susan and Mary's individual tragedies had been years apart, there is an emotional bond between those who live through the agony of premature death. When they met for the first time, Mary surprised Susan by complimenting her on the "Blood on the Cabbage" series.

"Boy, did I catch hell for that."

"I understood."

Mary gave Susan technical advice, but more importantly, she helped give Susan perspective on her role as an artist about to create a large mural in a public place. The gist of the conversation over several cups of coffee was, they were Corpus Christi artists. Every town, large and small, had their local artists who, for better or for worse, were a part of where they lived and took their inspiration. When being introduced or talked about by the local press, they would be described as "a well-known local artist," not "an internationally acclaimed artist whose work is currently on display at the Museum of Modern Art in New York City."

At length, they discussed Susan's vision of a mural that would tell a history of Corpus Christi, a relatively young seaport town in south Texas located 150 miles south of San Antonio. Mary liked Susan's idea of a WPA epic-style composition using jacked-up Mexican colors rather than earthy Midwestern tones. The old Bascule Bridge, which once connected downtown to North Beach—where prostitutes, gaming houses, and tattoo parlors were the main attractions—would be a ghost-like image behind the Breakers Hotel, the only building to survive the tidal wave of 1918. Between the ever-changing sand dunes on Padre Island were bleached bare-wood bait and tackle shacks that, along with cotton fields, oil rigs, and shrimp boats, were part of the essence she was trying to capture.

After drawing a final rendition in chalk on large sheets of paper taped to the bank floor, the next step was to calculate the areas and decide on the colors using samples.

After the one-inch-square colored-glass mosaic tiles arrived, the real art work began when she adhered the tiles to the wall—concentrating, looking at the drawings—walking back and looking at what had been done—deciding on what to do next. Then, once the mosaics were in place on the wall, the space in between the tiles had to be filled with a white, cement derivative called "grout"—a messy, tedious process involving water, buckets and sponges.

Completed by the end of the summer, the bank opening was a grand affair on the Corpus Christi social scale. Dressed to kill in an elegant evening gown, Charlie by her side, loved every single compliment dished out by those who had been invited to the champagne event. Invariably, when the others shook her hand, they were surprised by its coarseness.

Jeffrey entered Hamlin Junior High School the same year Susan began her new job as head of the University of Corpus Christi Art Department that had recently affiliated with Texas A & M. She hated leaving Del Mar Junior College, but this was a better facility with an expanded art curriculum. Nervousness, the new responsibilities, and a scheduling snafu, led to a rather interesting situation Susan solved single-handedly.

"How was your day, Charlie? Mine was one of those."

They were standing in the kitchen getting dinner ready while Jeff was in his room theoretically doing his homework and not watching the tube.

"Not bad. How about you?"

"I'm not sure. Strange. My model didn't show up when she was supposed to, leaving me with 15 students ready for their first life drawing class of the year, and there's ... no one to draw."

"Hum."

"So I decided to be the model."

"Good for you."

"I undressed ... I let the class draw me.

"Wait a second, Susan. You took off your clothes in front of the whole class? They all saw you?"

"I wasn't real excited about it either, but they needed a model. So, what the heck, I went for it."

"Susan, I can't believe this. All your clothes in front of a bunch of college kids?"

"Charlie, it's a life drawing class. We draw nudes. I am trying to teach these people how to draw the human body ... Charlie, I was their model not a stripper."

"How could you do this to me?"

"Do what to you?"

"How do you think I feel? Now, they all know what you look like without your clothes on. I've always felt that was my job—looking at you without your clothes on. I never expected my wife would be posing naked without asking me."

"Oh, Charlie, grow up. This is an art class I'm talking about."

"Isn't learning fun?"

"*Yes, it is.* There is an interesting woman in the class."

"Was she naked, too?"

"Charlie, it's no big deal."

"Susan, I suppose I pictured the Director of an Art Department as someone with her clothes on."

"Charlie, I'm trying to tell you about someone I have in my class. She's quite a character and her drawings aren't bad."

"No wonder you like her."

"Please stop, Charlie. All I did was provide the class with a human body to draw, which is not a serious crime in my book. I've invited this woman I'm trying to tell you about, and her husband over for drinks this weekend. I said I'd check with you and call."

"We can all take our clothes off and draw each other's human form, right?"

"Okay, that does it. I don't care if we do take all our clothes off, but you are going to come to my next life drawing class tomorrow at four o'clock. If you're not there, I swear to God I'll come get you at the office naked as the day I was born. You'll probably have to bail me out of jail. Don't you even try to argue."

And that was how Charlie met Red, Susan's new friend, for the first time. The day before she and her husband were to come over for drinks, Red was drawing naked people. The model who was scheduled the day before showed up along with the model who was supposed to pose that day. Rather than send him back home, the class had both a male and a female model.

At first, when they disrobed, Charlie felt out-of-place yet kind of cool looking at two young people totally undressed. He could see her every pubic hair and crinkle in her nipple. Feeling a tingle in his drawers thinking about his wife in the same pose, he tried to look serious as he glanced over the shoulders of students he was meeting for the first time. Drawing the live models in charcoal, Susan helped them learn how to draw arms, legs, faces, bosoms, and peckers. No one was lusting or drooling, and

Charlie had to admit that after a couple of minutes, he could see that the students really were diligently trying to interpret these figures on their sketch pads. It was erotic, but it wasn't what Charlie expected, nor was it easy.

"Red"—that's what everyone called her because her hair was the reddest Charlie had ever seen, and there was plenty of it. She had enrolled in Susan's creative and life drawing classes because she was anxious to try something new and this was titillating.

During the evening they had drinks together, the subject of nudity, not surprisingly, came up and Hal offered that Red had made him go to a nude beach when they were out in California.

"Hell, I'll confess—I wanted to see what it was like myself. Here were our kids, visiting their grandmother in Cuero, while their parents were parading around 'nekked.' Well, not really parading around. Red here took off her bathing suit like it was nothing. Now me, I lay down in the sand on my stomach and kind of wriggled out of my old boxer bathing suit. We were trying to act like this is something we did every day. What was funny was it didn't matter much what we looked like because, when I looked around, not a soul was paying the least bit of attention.

"That was just before a couple came and laid their beach blanket about 20 feet from us. They took off their shorts and tops and then, if you can believe this, they stood on their heads. That's when I knew I was seeing what people mean when they say things like, 'Only in California.' Seeing gravity pull upside down on things that are normally right side up was the highlight of our venture into the California culture. She was good-looking, too.

"Here Red had been giving me trouble about my hang-ups before we even found the beach. Then once we got there, we were right next to a couple whose every-things were hanging up. I got her on that one."

Chapter XII

Robstown

MR. and Mrs. Charlie Jones were on the Corpus Christi Social Scene "A" list and had friends and business contacts over to 3140 Ocean Drive often. Corpus Christi was where they were born so they knew everyone. Those runny nose, goofy kids running around the neighborhood barefoot were now grown-ups.

Yet, over time, it was Red and Hal's place in Robstown that became a refuge. As grand as Charlie and Susan's home was, they enjoyed getting away from the city every now and then. The countryside in the winter, a fire burning in the family room, it felt good to snuggle back in a "Ranch Style" living room chair, socialize and watch a football game on a TV in a "Ranch Style" cabinet.

The afternoon Red made sushi (causing everyone to almost hurt themselves laughing) was the first time Charlie began noticing how many magazines and books about boats Hal had lying around the living room. On the coffee table were: *Yachting, Wooden Boat, Cruising World*. In the bookshelves were books by the Hiscocks about circumnavigating and fitting out sailing yachts.

"Oh, I just like to read 'em. I started looking at the boats in Corpus years ago.

"Did you know there is a yellow 'junk' on the T-head called the *Lydia Pinkum*? I asked around and there used to be a diarrhea cure called Lydia Pinkum's something or other. The old man who lives on board is a recluse. As often as I go down there, I've caught a glimpse of him and his cat only once. For pure entertainment, there's nothing better than the magazine articles about young couples with stars in their eyes talking about the 'cruising life' — sailing-off-into-the-sunset written all over their smiles. It's quite a notion.

"I go down to the boatyard, Laguna Madre Marine, every time I'm in the neighborhood and check out what's going on. There are rich men and boat bums all in a little boat society. Everyone has their druthers, and everyone knows what they're talking about—just ask them—the fiberglass boaters think the wooden boaters are impractical purists. The wooden boaters affectionately call fiberglass boats Clorox bottles. Germans all have steel boats.

"The fact is wood rots, steel rusts, fiberglass breaks down and blisters."

Their everyday friendship and cozy camaraderie is why there was so much concern when Susan and Charlie found out that Hal was in the hospital after collapsing on a rig one September afternoon.

Several weeks later, after they'd gotten the results from the tests back, Charlie did not have a good feeling when Hal asked to meet him at his office.

"Charlie, the doctors are pretty certain I have a brain aneurysm brought on by the mild stroke I had last month. Red and I have checked with the best doctors in the field, and the prognosis isn't very good if that's what I have. The consensus is, no one knows exactly how long I've got. It could be two days or 20 years before this weakened membrane is going to let go in my head, and I am going to be dead, like that," he snapped his fingers.

"The actuaries say two years, which seems like a long time in a way and a short time in another way. I am 70-years-old, so I have lived a fairly long life I suppose, but it sure went by fast. It seems like yesterday I was a cowboy roughneck drinking beer in a dance hall and I see this redhead stuffed into her blue jeans. It was like getting shocked when I put my arm around her waist. How can that one person out of all the rest hit you like a bolt of lightning?"

"Let's take a walk, Hal. Let's get out of here for a while," Charlie said as he wrote a note to his secretary. Normally, Charlie was comfortable in his walnut-paneled office overlooking the harbor and the T-heads, but on hearing Hal's news, he immediately got a lump in his throat the size of a grapefruit. A walk might help.

Before they left, he took off his coat and tie and carelessly put them on a chair and didn't even bother picking them up when they slid off the polished leather seat.

Silently, they waited for the elevator that took them to the ground floor. After pushing through the heavy, Art Deco-inspired stainless steel revolving door with oval-etched glass, they walked down the quarter-moon-shaped cement steps that separated "Uptown" from "Downtown." Uptown, on the bluff, was primarily offices buildings and parking garages. Most of the retail stores were Downtown, closer to the water.

Passing Kelly's Men's Shoes and a woman's apparel store, they walked toward the T-head, crossing Ocean Drive. Still cool from the air conditioning, the sticky heat would take several minutes before it had an effect on them.

Charlie and Hal could have gone to the yacht club, but chose a wood park bench facing the water and the familiar 20-knot wind that was blowing across Corpus Christi Bay. Barely noticing the familiar salt water/seaweed smell, their faces moistened from the humid air as their shirts stuck to their chests.

Hal's hair was thin on top. The wrinkles around his eyes were molded by the days he had spent under the Texas sun out in the countryside with quail, rabbits, snakes, deer and oil wells. His hands weren't rough the way they used to be, but the work he had done throughout his life had shaped them. Charlie looked at his own and saw how straight his fingers were compared to Hal's curved thick fingers that rested on his knee—workin' hands.

"I have made quite a bit of money, Charlie. For a nobody to have come as far as I have, it still surprises me," he said matter-of-factly.

"The money part is where I want you to come in. I don't want Red or the kids to have to worry too much about it when my time comes. Don't worry, she's good with money, but if you could take care of the death stuff? You know what I'm talking about."

"Hal, what are you supposed to do? Are you supposed to take it easy?"

"Well the good news is I'm not dead yet. It's easy to get sad and worried. I haven't even told the children. I will when the time's right.

"I can do normal things, but my days of hard labor are over.

"Red and I have decided to buy ourselves a van and take a trip up the East Coast. We want to visit our older boy in Miami—get out of town for a while. I am dying to see the Yankee boats.

"I know you'll tell Susan. Quite frankly, I don't want to talk about this again because realistically, I could live to be 100....

"You'll do this for me won't you, Charlie?"

Charlie took Hal's outstretched hand in his own and held onto it for a few seconds before putting his arm around him like a Latino. "Of course," and, with Charlie's right hand on Hal's shoulder, they slowly began their walk back to the Driscoll parking garage.

Chapter XIII

Par for the Course

"THAT was a hell of a shot you made on the 14th, Charlie. I thought it was a hole-in-one. For not having played in a while, I'd say 93 was damn good. I think my problem is not letting my hips move through the ball before my hands. For some reason, I keep bending my left knee too much when I rotate the club on my back swing. It causes me to lose power and hit down into the ball too much. I hit the ball so fat on the 11th, I was afraid I'd knocked a filling loose. Thank God it went past the ladies' tee, or I'd have had to play that hole with my dick hanging out."

Bud, an oil man, was one of the regular Saturday

golfers Charlie had been playing with.

"Have you been to Neiman-Marcus lately? Charlie, I'm telling you—could you put a patch on this drink, Charlie? I need it after Dallas—I couldn't believe how much things have gone up. Last weekend we flew up in McNeal's Twin Bonanza. Hell of an airplane. I don't know what all Lauren bought, but we had to ship half of it back. Those two women bought so much, we couldn't fit it in the plane—and that's a six-seater.

"Part of it was a lamp Lauren had to have that looks like a giraffe. I kept asking her, where are we going to put a giraffe lamp? Made in Africa, Algeria, some damn place."

Rain was beating against the living room windows that Juan washed every day due to the salt air. Downtown was barely visible as Charlie turned on more inside lights and fixed another Scotch for Bud and himself. Susan brought in some mixed nuts, and the "gals," with their wine, joined the men.

Lauren—the sun was beginning to take its toll on her dark, overly tanned skin—continued the conversation she and Susan had been having in the kitchen. "I hear the Lawrence children are awfully upset with their father. Look what he's done to the family. Isn't that the way it always goes? He wasn't playing patty-cake with that girl around the corner, either. Katie is *furious*. If I found out ol' Bud here was doing that to me, I'd string him up by the you-know-whats. And you stop laughing, Bud. It is not funny."

"Oh, Lauren. He just liked to stay up a little later than she did," Bud said, and winked at Charlie. Lauren, blue eyes highlighted with blue mascara, hit Bud on the leg with her fist.

Almost everyone in Corpus Christi knows almost everything, and everyone knew about Lewis Lawrence's escapades except his wife, Katie, who acted cute/dumb, maybe as a shield to escape the reality of what was going on behind her back.

Numb to Bud's voice, Charlie's mind drifted to Hal, his health and the van packed to the brim with some of the oddest things—in case they needed them. They'd been gone for over a month now, and Susan and Charlie both missed the two or three visits a week Red made to the house to chat and to see what Susan was up to in her corner. Rarely staying long, she was always full of it and downright funny. Hal who came by less often, was the perfect straight man.

"I'll bet you do, too, don't you Charlie?"

"Sometimes he does and sometimes he doesn't," Susan interrupted when she realized that her husband hadn't heard a word they were saying.

When they finally got Lauren and Bud out to their car under umbrellas, Susan apologized for inviting them over. She told Charlie about Lauren's invitation to drive out to the club for a swim where they could keep an eye out for the men coming up the 18th fairway and meet them for a drink after the round.

An unexpected thunderstorm forced Charlie, Bud, and the rest of the foursome to hurry the last hole to beat the rain. In an effort to be sociable, Susan suggested she and Bud come over on their way home.

"What's wrong Charlie? For a change, I was trying to invite the right kind of people over."

"Susan, it's me. I've been listening to Bud all afternoon. The truth is, I can't get Hal and Red off my mind. The other truth is, I am having a hard time telling Lew I can't represent him. I'm not a divorce lawyer. Lauren was talking about stringing Bud up by the balls if she caught him; well, that is exactly what Katie Lawrence is trying her best to do to Lew. Maybe we need a vacation. Where would you like to go? Hawaii? Back to France?"

"Maybe Italia. What does Lew have to say about it?"

"He's miserable. The kids are so mad they won't even speak to him. He's begged and pleaded with Katie to forgive him, but I don't think she will—everybody cries and everybody's sorry after they get caught.

"It was her money that got him started. She put up the money for the car dealership in the first place, and she's mad. She wants revenge."

"Hi Mom. Hi Dad," Jeffrey said as he wandered into the living room and plopped down on the white sofa. Susan and Charlie knew their son couldn't have been eavesdropping because no one could possibly hear anything over the stereo blasting in his room. Jeffrey was wearing his trademark green Keds high-top tennis shoes without socks. Underneath scraggly whiskers were several red pimples with whiteheads. Below the baggy shirt and shorts, the lower part of his legs had gotten hairy. Charlie looked at the kid and thought he looked more like a space alien than his own flesh and blood.

Before the rain, Jeff had been skateboarding in the church parking lot. Theoretically, since then, he had been studying in his room.

"How's the homework coming, Jeff? I'm serious about getting those grades up and reading more."

"Oh, I'm finished. Could we order a pizza? There's nothing to eat around here. I'm starved."

"Jeff, stay here with your father while I fix something for all of us. You had pizza last night and that junk is so hard on your complexion. Have you been using the cream at night?"

Charlie could see that Jeff had just finished a grape soda because his teeth had a yellow/purple tint to them.

"How was golf, Dad? You win?"

"No, I didn't play badly, though. How's the reading going? I don't see how you can concentrate with all that racket."

"It's easy, Dad. It's not racket. You had your music when you were growing up."

"What books have you read?"

"I finished *House of Scarlet Horrors* last week."

"Jeff, you are going to be a sophomore in high school next year. You ought to be reading something more mature."

"But I like scary books. I thought you said I could read whatever I wanted to as long as I was reading something, then you get all mad because I have a *Playboy*, big deal. I'll bet you looked at it after you took it away. I'll bet you anything."

Charlie still had the magazine in one of his dresser drawers.

"Steinbeck, have you read any of his books? *The Grapes of Wrath*? Surely, you're supposed to read that one. *Playboy* is not a good influence on someone your age, Jeff. Sex is not the only thing there is, you know. What would you think of your mother and I if we subscribed to the *Playboy* philosophy? At your age, I don't think I even knew what sex was," which was a big fat lie that Jeff acknowledged sarcastically with a purple-tooth grin.

"I hear your friend Mr. Lawrence is sure having fun."

"Jeffrey, I don't know what you've heard, but Mr. and Mrs. Lawrence are very upset and the children are caught in the middle."

"He didn't look upset when I saw him going into the Six Points Pharmacy with that girl. Man, you should have seen her 'daisy dukes,' great ass. Good you-know-what's, too," Jeff said with another irritating purple grin.

"There's no reason to talk like that, son. Are you, uh? You could ruin your life if you got a girl pregnant. Is there anything you want to talk to me about? Do you have any questions about anything?"

"Yeah, Dad, could I go to the KISS concert Tuesday night if I get my homework done first? I know it's a school night, but they're pretty cool. None of the really cool bands come to Corpus Christi. There's nothing to do around here that's any fun. The tickets are only $15. We're all going to meet out front before we go in."

"I'll talk it over with your mother. Let's go see what she's up to," said a defeated Charlie. "Don't you want to shave that fuzz, Jeff? You look so damn sloppy. They let you go to school like that? Maybe you could get a haircut," was thrown in as an afterthought to a conversation that had gone nowhere except a KISS concert. Jeff was his and Susan's Number One topic of conversation these days. She kept saying how awkward the age he was going through can be. At one point Charlie even suggested military school.

"He's only in the ninth grade, Charlie."

A lot of Charlie's frustrations were the result of his own work habits. The family saw each other briefly at breakfast during the school year. Not much was discussed during the hurried ritual. Susan usually picked Jeff up from junior high. After divulging next to nothing about his school day, he would go out with his skateboard to hang out until dinner. Later, without saying much, he went to his room to do his homework with the TV on.

As often as not, Jeffrey was hungry and ate before Susan and Charlie, because Charlie liked to have a drink or two when he got home from the office, sometimes as late as 6 or 6:30.

Charlie didn't lead a dual sex life, but he did lead a dual life between office and home. At the office, where he spent most of his waking hours, he was King. "Yes, Mr. Jones. Anything else, Mr. Jones?" There was order.

Charlie enjoyed coming home, but the atmosphere

was 180 degrees. Invariably, the phone started ringing the minute Jeff walked through the front door, interrupting any intelligent conversation that might possibly take place. When they did talk, Jeff had a way of starting arguments with his flippant know-it-all asides about things he truly knew little or nothing about. Routinely, Susan checked his written homework, and Charlie looked over his math.

"Jeffrey, go brush your teeth."

Charlie couldn't take the grape soda, purple teeth for a second longer.

"Aw, Dad we're about to eat. Can't I do it afterwards? It'll make the food taste funny."

"Jeffrey, *go brush your teeth.*"

Chapter XIV

Back with a Plan

JOLTED out of a trance by the loud ring, Susan picked up the paint-smeared beige receiver of her rotary telephone that sat on top of a paint-smeared wicker table and heard that familiar voice. "Red, you're back! How are you?" Susan said as she pulled her ankles up underneath her on the paint-blotched sofa and snuggled back into the cushions.

"We're a little road punchy, but fine other than that. Got home last night. We thought about stopping by on our way into town, but didn't know what you were up to, and we'd driven all the way from Atlanta. That van of ours is something else. We could sleep and switch driving. We pulled off the road and just slept for a while a couple of times. I'll tell you what, it is good to be home."

"We missed you. I think Charlie's been worrying about you and Hal. Charlie worries as well as anyone. He's been touchy lately."

"Listen, Susan, if you don't have any plans this weekend, Hal and I would love to take you hunting. He talked about quail all the way home. We ate some wonderful food, a lot of seafood, but on the way back, he craved the taste of quail cooked on an open grill with a piece of bacon wrapped around it. That and Tex/Mex food.

"Harlequin #1 is up near Alice. The farmer's land he's drilling on has invited us to use his dogs and an old Bronco he customized for hunting. We thought you could drive up early Saturday morning and hunt with us, and then we could come back to here and cook out. We've got some news for you."

After a long conversation, the plan evolved. They'd ask Ivory and Evett and they'd make Jeff come along. Travel-wise, it would be better if everyone came back to Corpus Christi and put the quail on the grill by the pool. Red and Hal would stay the night in the guest bedroom so they didn't have to drive back to Robstown after what surely would be a long day.

The air was crisp as the Joneses drove in the morning darkness. Normally, women do not go on hunting trips, but Red, thanks to her dad, was a better shot than Hal. Jim, their spoiled indoor bird dog, was in the truck.

Bojangles—Charlie, Susan, and Jeff's two-year-old Irish Setter—got to come, too. Though he'd never been hunting before, he wouldn't be gun-shy because they often shot a blank pistol while he ate his food to get him used to the sound.

The back of Susan's latest station wagon was packed with hunting jackets, shotguns, rattlesnake guards, shotgun shells, coolers filled with drinks and sandwiches.

They met Red and Hal at a crowded, noisy, early morning cafe in Alice where the only other women were waitresses. The rest were men, sitting with one leg crossed over the other at the knee, smokin', drinkin' coffee and talkin' farm talk—the kind of men who woke up at five o'clock every morning of their lives—the high point of their day being cigarettes and coffee as the sun came up.

After a big breakfast, Charlie followed Hal's El Camino out of Alice and down a dirt road with two barbed wire gates that Red held open for both cars. The lights going up the derrick of Harlequin #1 were still visible as the dawn of a new day was breaking.

None of the Joneses had ever been on the platform of a rig before, so Hal took them up the steel steps where they gathered under the covered area off to the side of the vibrating platform floor. First, he explained how drilling "mud" was pumped from the open pit beside the derrick into the drilling pipe, providing enough weight to keep the well from blowing out if they struck oil. He was shouting over the diesel motors as he explained that they were about to add a 30-foot stand of pipe.

As they watched, the roughnecks threw chocks around the pipe that was in the ground to hold it in place. Then, a four-foot-long wrench called a "tong"—so heavy it's suspended from the derrick by a steel cable—was clamped around the stand of pipe about five or six inches from the top.

This is the part that was fascinating:

Before the new stand of pipe was added, a roughneck wrapped a chain (coming from a mechanical wench next to the driller) around the top of the pipe *four* times. After the new stand of pipe was "stabbed" into place, the roughneck flipped the chain so that it crawled up to the new stand of pipe. Then, as the driller pulled on the chain, the new pipe would spin its threads into the lower one. Finally, it was tightened with the other set of tongs and another 30 feet was on its way into the ground. Keep in mind Hal pointed out, it is the 7-inch diameter pipe itself that is rotating two miles underneath the earth's surface.

According to Red, the word "roughneck" originated long before oil rigs and referred to men who were rough, violent, rude and uncivilized. It evolved to mean men who pursue "risky, physically demanding occupations," which fit the early oil rig workers like a glove.

Back in their cars, they drove the remaining mile to the farmhouse where the Bronco and farmer's dogs were waiting.

After a good hunt, back at 3140 Ocean Drive everyone was resting except Red and Susan. They had too much to catch up on.

"Red, Hal looks good. Is he doing all right?"

"I think so. His first reaction was to go out and prove he could still do everything the way he's always done them. The next phase, thankfully, was realizing it was okay to take things easier. Supervise a little more and do a little less. Wait 'till you hear what he's up to this time. I'm in favor of it as long as he follows my rules.

"I'm not going to steal his thunder, but Susan, Hal's turned into a boat nut. Looking at boats is what we did on our whole trip. Now, he wants to build one. I won't let him do the actual building, just supervise. He's got several men who would be good at it. As he philosophically pointed out to me, 'Because the bunch of us doesn't know a damn thing about building a boat is no reason we shouldn't be allowed to try if we want to.'"

After rinsing the birds and putting them in a "Mojo" marinade Ivory had concocted the night before, they put baking potatoes in the oven. The corn in the shuck could go on the grill. Later on, they could make a salad. It would be a good excuse to get away from the men if they wanted to.

As the sun dropped in the sky and they began getting their second wind, Hal had a bourbon and Coke. Charlie a Scotch, and Ivory a beer with a shot of tequila. The girls had white wine—a nice bottle of Pinot Grigio.

"It was a hell of a trip. If either of you want to borrow the van, I highly recommend it.

"We decided to drive down the Overseas Highway, along the railroad tracks of Flagler's Overseas Railroad, to Key West. We'd never seen water so beautiful. It's a rebellious type place that put even more ideas in Hal's head.

"Miami was okay, but we were glad to get out of the big city and wander up the coast on the back roads and small towns. The seafood's as good in Florida as it is here in Texas."

Red was ready for him to get to the good parts. "Tell 'em about the Yankees."

"Well, of all the boats we saw, I'll have to admit, I was impressed by the design of Yankee boats—built for weather. One thing gave us a good laugh. Did you know there is a duck that inhabits the Northeast Coast called a 'Harlequin'? Beautiful little ducks.

"It was up East that I got to see some of the most interesting boats I have ever seen. In fact, it was in a little outdoor place in Newport, Rhode Island, overlooking the harbor that I told Red what I wanted to do. She said she had pretty much figured out where this was going.

"Okay folks. This is it. *We are going to build our own boat.*"

"Hang on Hal, I want to hear all about this," Charlie said as he took a break to replenish their drinks and tend the grill. It was a beautiful evening—without wind for a change—so they set up the table like a buffet with mountains of corn on the cob, bacon-wrapped quail, salad, jalapeño cornbread, pinto beans, and hot sauce. There were plenty of places for everyone to sit and eat overlooking the calm bay and the lights that were beginning to reflect on the water.

One lesson Hal was learning. No one starts jumping up and down clapping, "Bravo, what a wonderful idea," when they are told someone is going to build their own boat. An "okay, that's an interesting idea" look appears on their faces as they nod their heads absentmindedly, slowly up and down. People don't quite know how to react.

Ivory's ears perked up immediately when he heard the news.

Chapter XV

Across a Crowded Room

THE weekend after the hunting party, Jeff was, kind of invited to a party himself. With nothing else to do, he went over to Chuck's house with a case of Old Milwaukee and put the cans in one of the coolers in the backyard.

Inside, cigarette smoke permeated the game room filled with high school boys and girls.

Chuck, the host, was having a premonition that this big-shot idea of his was a fiasco in the making and that he was surely going to get caught for throwing a party while his folks were away. How did so many people find out? Hopefully, no one would spill beer on the carpet or burn the couch or who knew what else.

In fact, Chuck was learning by the minute that throwing an unauthorized party was nowhere near as much fun as being a happy-go-lucky guest. A subconscious voice was whispering that his parents were going to go ballistic— "How could you do this to us? Didn't we tell you specifically not to have friends over? Do you know what could have happened if someone, God forbid, had been hurt going home? How do you expect us to ever trust you when you deliberately disobey?"

Even if he did manage to get things cleaned up and deodorized, someone was bound to say something. It seemed as though the whole school was there, including some weird-ass skateboarders.

Jeff looked like a typical "boarder." His long shorts were so low on his hips that anyone looking at him from behind could see the top of his crack outlined in a T-shirt that said, "YEAH RIGHT" on the back. Feeling the rush of smoking his first joint and drinking an ice-cold beer, he immediately saw her as she came in through the front door.

Wearing a short white tank top, he could see her white brassiere through the slightly transparent cotton cloth. Though her long legs were tan and athletic and her rear exquisitely round, it was her smile that had him thinking, *"Ohhh, Jeffrey, you could fall for a girl like that,"* —not that he had the slightest chance in the world. She was a varsity cheerleader dating *the* Corpus Christi star halfback.

Ambling around, Jeff pitched the empty into a trash can and walked outside to the ice chest. Popping his second, he sat beside Chuck's Golden Retriever and began rubbing his ears and talking to him. As the dog rolled over on his back, Lynn, the girl that had caught Jeff's eye, came up from behind, startling him.

"Hi."

She sat down on her knees and began patting the dog's neck. Unbelievably pretty, he thought as he looked at the side of her face while she affectionately rubbed the dog's chest—his fuzzy white thing and balls cutely on display.

"Uh, hi," was all he could think of to say.

"We had to put ours to sleep last week," she said as tears formed in her blue-gray eyes surrounded with mascara. "I'm sorry," she said as she wiped her cheek with the back of her hand. "I've never lost anything I've loved before."

"Me too," was all Jeff could manage before recovering with, "I'm sorry...."

"When I was younger we had to do that to ours, too" regaining some composure. That a varsity cheerleader would come up and make conversation with him was not something he'd expected.

"What's your name?"

"Jeff, Jeff Jones, I'm a junior."

"You're a boarder, right?

"What's *that* like?"

At school the skateboarders were a social caste all their own. They were into weed and asphalt parking lots—the rebels, the losers.

"I don't know," he shrugged. "It's pretty cool."

"What do your parents think? My dad would have a cow if someone came to the door with an earring. He's pretty out of it. Could I have a beer?"

"Sure," Jeff said as he opened the cooler, pulled one out of the icy water and opened it before handing it to her.

"Well, I'd better get back inside, Todd will be wondering where I am. See ya," she said before hesitating to pet the dog goodbye.

Not knowing what to say or do, wanting to make some kind of an impression, Jeff inexplicably, out of the blue, said, "Wait." He took the gold loop out of his earlobe and put it in her hand.

Her hands were so soft and smooth and pretty. Walking off, looking back at him with an ever-so-slight smile, she put it in her pocket and walked toward the door.

Jeff couldn't believe how dumb he felt as he chugged his beer and opened another. Might as well get wasted now that he'd made a fool of himself.

Driving home in his mother's station wagon, he had to keep one eye closed to keep from seeing double. Nothing reckless, no peeling out or anything, his total concentration was staying on the road. At the second intersection, he turned a little too early, running over the curb scraping the bottom of the car. The sound of metal against concrete sobered him up slightly—enough to get home.

Pulling into the circular driveway, his thoughts staggered back to the girl whose hand he'd touched when he'd given her the earring. At this point, he was drunk enough to think it was a brilliantly suave move. Lurching toward the front door, he could see the lights were on inside—this could be bad. Shit, the car lights were still on. He muffled the sound of a belch and tried to clear his head as he went back to the car, opened the door and pushed in the headlight switch, inadvertently hitting the turn signal, which was now blinking orange.

"Jeff, is that you?" his dad said as he opened the large carved, varnished walnut front door. Standing in his robe on the polished marble entranceway, Charlie Jones could see that his 17-year-old son was smashed. Trying hard not to blow his top, he could smell beer on his only child's breath and smoke on his clothes. Though Jeff couldn't focus well, he was aware that his mother, in her robe, had joined his dad as they pulled him inside and closed the door.

"Where in the hell have you been?"

Jeff shrugged without saying anything.

"Do you know it's after two o'clock in the morning?"

Jeff was trying with all his being to appear sober, but his body wasn't cooperating. It wouldn't work right.

"You'd be in jail now if the police had stopped you," Charlie said through clenched teeth, "could have killed someone," the muscles in his temples flexed as his jaw tightened.

When his dad commanded, "Stand still, put your finger to your nose," Jeff cavalierly poked himself in the eye. *Ouch.* Covering the eye with both hands, he tried to walk toward his room. Because he was standing on one of his untied green high-top tennis shoelaces, his body lunged forward while his right foot stayed in the same place causing him to fall hard on the carpeted hallway. Susan and Charlie disgustedly followed the sequence offering no help to their pathetic son who used the wall to help himself up, leaving fingerprints smudges on the beige paint.

"Be better, promise," Jeff muttered as he made the right turn to his room still holding his eye. The flashing blinker of the car could be seen through the semi-transparent curtains covering the full-length windows in the hallway.

No way could Charlie or Susan get to sleep now. Charlie turned off the turn signal, poured a Scotch and a wine and carried them back to the bedroom.

"What a jerk," he said to Susan as he handed her the wine. "It's a wonder he made it home.

"This time there are going to be some changes made. Car privileges are out. I'm taking that fucking skateboard of his and throwing it in the garbage can. Seventeen-years-old coming home like that."

Susan, who usually tried to defend Jeff, was just as upset. Not even bothering to remind Charlie that he, too, had driven home drunk. She shook her head saying, "I know, I know, you're right, Charlie."

"It's not too late to get him into a private school. That may be the way to go. He's rude. He doesn't listen at all. Our wonderful, dear son is an asshole," he said as he angrily turned out the bedside lamp. Neither he nor Susan would sleep well as they, butt-to-butt, quietly stared at the darkened room, trying to figure out the right thing to do.

Jeff awakened to the bright sunlight pouring in

through the sliding glass doors of his bedroom because he'd forgotten to close the curtains. His head wasn't merely throbbing, it was pounding, and it was doubtful there was any aspirin in his medicine cabinet. "Ten-thirty," he saw on the clock as he walked, holding his head, to the bathroom, where he lowered himself onto the commode.

Trying to remember the night before, his first reaction was to convince himself that he wasn't in trouble. His right eye looked a little puffy in the large bathroom mirror. The black hole in his memory was trying to fight off vague images of his parents greeting him at the door. *Oh man.* Where the hell was his earring, he wondered as he pushed back his tangled long hair from the front of his unshaven face? Oh no. Why had he given it to that girl, Lynn? What an idiot. What a total fucking idiot. Why would anyone give their earring to a girl they didn't know? *The pool. Get in the swimming pool.* His bathing suit was cold and damp from the day before.

In Bermuda shorts and a golf shirt, Charlie approached Jeff as he came up for air in the aqua colored water on a crystal-clear morning in October.

"Señor Borracho, if you wouldn't mind getting your sorry ass out of the pool and into the breakfast room, your mother and I would like to have a few words with you about teenage behavior."

No way to get out of this one. He showered and cut his chin shaving with a shaky hand. He gave up trying to stop the bleeding and left a patch of toilet paper on the nick, put on some of his less offensive clothes and walked, head hung low, wet stringy hair in his face, to the breakfast table.

The drone of Charlie's sermon about drinking and driving and drinking in general, and how scruffy he looked, and how stupid skateboarding was, and how what he had done was a reflection on the family, not to mention his future and how he needed to take responsibility for his actions, was literally going in one ear and out the other as Jeff tried to figure a way to get out of the house now that he wasn't going to be allowed to drive. Jeff, who thought his mom and dad were never going to shut up, was thinking about an escape and about Lynn, too much to even counterattack with the, "I'll bet you did the same thing when you were young," routine. Forcing his eggs and bacon down, "haircut" popped up like a cue card in his mind.

Charlie was so caught off guard by Jeff's seemingly sincere apologies and his offer to get a haircut that both he and Susan backed off some, deciding that he could drive during the day. He couldn't drive at night for two weeks, and Charlie insisted, "Plan on staying home tonight," Saturday night. "Whatever," thought Jeff, "Just let me out of here—Alka-Seltzer—if I can just find an Alka-Seltzer." The burning in his stomach was so severe he could taste breakfast in his throat.

Charlie and Susan knew how bad he felt, and it made them glad. "Charlie, is it my imagination or was that awful earring gone?"

For Jeff, being home alone on a Saturday night was a total drag. Still not feeling his best, he stayed in his room watching wrestling for a while, then a made-for-TV-movie entitled, *Up Your Uzi.*

Sunday was a much, much brighter day. He looked up her number in the phone book and pushed the buttons.

"Lynn?"

"Yes?"

"This is Jeff." There was a silence on the other end of the phone making him think she didn't remember him. "Jeff Jones, I was petting the dog Friday night."

"Hi, Jeff," she said as she thought about the night before, "want your earring back?" she teased—*awfully bold of him calling her on the phone!*

"No, 'cause if I wore it your dad wouldn't let me take you out," he countered.

"I don't think Todd or my dad is going to think that's a good idea."

"I cut my hair, and you've got the earring."

Jeff told her about the trouble he was in at home. They compared notes on parental stupidity and parents in general for a half an hour or so before he popped the big question, "Lynn, not like a date or anything, but I thought maybe you would like to come with me when I take my dog to the beach? Bojangles is an Irish Setter, and he loves to run in the surf. Maybe keep me company for an hour or two seeing how I can't go out at night."

"I doubt it, but I'll think about it, Jeff. Just friends, Jeff, okay?" She missed her old dog and that was the only reason she even considered the offer—her poor, gone dog.

Conversation came easy as they talked for another half an hour before Lynn had to hang up. Having been nicked by Cupid's arrow a couple of times, Jeff had the feeling this was a serious wound that was probably going to cause him even more trouble than his previous brushes with love.

Things were confusing to the point that Jeff was unable to concentrate when he talked to his current, sorta, girlfriend who regularly phoned him or vice versa.

Marilyn was a skater's girl and the first girl he had made love with—no big deal, what's a fuck between friends—was how it began. Real sex sure beat loping the mule, but there was a problem: once you started, you became attached. He'd have to deal with that.

Lynn was all he could think about—so easy to talk too, so smart, and her voice was like velvet with a laugh so genuine coming from deep in her throat. Jeff was constantly daydreaming and calculating how to go about making her fall in love with him and leaving her stupid halfback standing in his stinky, sweat-stained football uniform, crying in the rain.

As it was, his fellow boarders were going to tease him ruthlessly about going straight now that he had given up his earring and gotten about half of his hair cut off. It was still respectably long, but if he combed it back instead of letting it hang in his face, he was tall, dark and handsome.

Was he going to turn his back on his friends and lover for this cheerleader girl? Yep. If he could. Perhaps not being able to go out nights for two weeks was going to work to his advantage. Charlie and Susan were suspiciously curious about why he was enduring the punishment so well. Something was going on, and they hadn't a clue.

Though the waiting about killed him, Jeff skipped a day before calling Lynn again. "No, Jeff, not this week." It wasn't right for her to go to the beach, not yet, perhaps the next Monday. It seemed sneaky to go somewhere with someone else without telling Todd, and she didn't want to go through that.

Not even their respective friends knew they were getting acquainted with each other over the phone because her friends were Todd's friends, and she didn't particularly want them to know. Jeff sure couldn't tell his parents or his boarder friends that he was a traitor talking to and falling hopelessly for a cheerleader. He compared himself and Lynn to "Running Bear and Little White Dove" who, in the stupid song he'd heard on the radio while driving with his mother, were on the opposite sides of a muddy river, wanting to get together yet unable to.

No longer did his parents' big house embarrass him. Now he wanted to show her that he was a somebody and one way was to let her know where he lived—3140 Ocean Drive. He also thought it might be a good time to pull out the clubs and play a round of golf, something he hadn't done in a while. Lynn's family, he found out, had recently joined the Corpus Christi Country Club and rumor had it that she was spending time at the pool without numbskull Todd. That would be a good place to run into each other.

Susan and Charlie were in the dark trying to understand what was going on. Of course, Jeff hadn't told them about her, and they weren't naive enough to think that he had listened to what they had said and that he was miraculously reforming his behavior for them. He was still grumpy and as secretive as ever, yet something was going on in his private life that was encouraging, and it was about time. Finding the weed stash (big blow-up) and the lousy grades (blowing off his homework) had left them feeling frustrated, helpless and mad.

"How come you live in that fancy house and drive this 'hooptie'?" Lynn said as she opened the door and seated herself in the passenger side of the dinged-up, 10-year-old station wagon.

Embarrassed, Jeff replied that it was his mother's, and she was kind of the nutty artist type who liked the old thing.

"I have a feeling that I am about to get in trouble. I can't believe you talked me into this, and don't you dare tell a soul. You promised. Todd would have a cow if he found out."

He wondered where she got this thing with cows. "I won't, I swear. I just wanted to talk and I knew you missed your dog and thought you might have fun throwing the Frisbee for Bojangles."

Wearing an extra-large T-shirt with W. B. Ray Varsity on the front and Todd's number 44 on the back, it was "Todd this" and "Todd that" all the way to the beach.

Thankfully, driving to Mustang Island didn't take long since they didn't have to wait for the floating causeways that open for boat traffic. By taking one of the access roads that cut through the sand dunes, Jeff could drive the car right onto the deserted beach where the wind roared and the breakers, one after another, relentlessly pounded the sand. In the distance, through the surf's mist, they could see the stilted white Coast Guard building on the point.

There weren't any people near a large piece of driftwood where they stopped. Opening the tailgate, Bojangles bolted for the ocean as Jeff and Lynn, looked at each other, shrugged as they pulled their shirts off and ran in the soft sand behind him.

Good God, Jeff thought as he saw her for the first time in her bright orange bikini. She was tan everywhere except a sliver of white skin that leaked from her top until she adjusted it slightly. She was perfect, absolutely perfect—her blond ponytail, threaded through the back of a baseball hat, waived behind her. Be cool, he repeated to himself. *Be cool.*

The roar of the ocean made it hard for them to talk much, but they did throw the Frisbee, and they became caught up in laughter with Bojangles as he was dunked time and time again by the surf before he invariably found the Frisbee in the foam and brought it back. Bo always waited until he was beside them before he shook the sand

and saltwater from his Irish red fur, causing her to turn to Jeff's chest to shield herself. Good dog.

After a brief swim in the surf, Lynn let him hold her finger playfully as they walked back to the car. "Thump, Thump, Thump," went his heartbeat as their eyes met again when he opened her door.

Susan and Charlie had never seen their son so upbeat and happy at dinner—what was going on here? He had been doing his homework, and he looked a 1,000% better than he had for an eternal year.

"What'd you do this afternoon, Jeff?

"Nothing Dad, Bo and I took a drive to the beach."

Drive to the beach Charlie thought? Jeff never takes the dog to the beach.

"Anyone go with you?"

"Nope, just me and Bo."

"Well?" said Susan to Charlie now that they were back in their bedroom, getting ready for bed. Charlie had just come from closing the garage door and making sure everything was locked.

"You're right, there was sand on the other side too. I wonder who he's seeing that's such a big secret?"

They couldn't believe how stupid children must think their parents are. Knowing Jeff wouldn't wipe the car seats with a towel, the discovery that there had been a passenger had been elementary. Also, there were several strands of long blond hair on the back of the car seat that were on the passenger side of the car.

For Jeff, the world looked like a wonderful place for a change. He ran into her at the club over the weekend wearing the same bathing suit, and they talked....

Conversely, it seemed like the whole world caved in on him the night she told him over the phone that she couldn't go to the beach with him again, and that he should stop calling. She liked him a lot she said, maybe a little too much she confided, but there was Todd. It was too dangerous, and they shouldn't be doing this behind his back. Jeff argued in vain that they weren't doing anything, but she held firm, leaving him with the receiver in the same hand that had briefly held her finger.

Discussing the return of the surly Jeff they had known so well, Susan confessed that she hadn't been able to find out a thing about this mystery woman and what had gone wrong.

Chapter XVI

Hurricane Greta

A lot adjacent to "Laguna Madre Marine" was where Hal chose to build the boat. The rent was reasonable and the marina's travel lift could easily go the short distance from the marina to the construction site when the time was right. The Intracoastal Waterway was close by.

Hal knew the south Texas sun and heat would be too much for them unless there was a roof over the worksite. That and the tools would need to be locked up at night so the first thing he did was bring a steel storage shed over from Harlequin Oil.

The hull itself had to be built upside down because laying heavy pieces of steel down on a framework is a lot easier than hoisting them up into place. Hal wanted gravity working for, not against, him. This, of course, meant the hull would eventually have to be turned over.

Thinking it would be a shame to build a shed, tear it down and build it again, Hal made the roof detachable with two big eye bolts on the top. That way the marina's travel lift could take off the roof, turn the hull over and put the roof back on. A picnic table was put under a tree next to the air-conditioned trailer Hal brought in.

Normally, hurricane season is over when the first cold front of the year blows through. But, this year a late, unexpected storm had gathered over warm water circulating in the Gulf of Mexico creating Hurricane Greta. There is a feeling of dread a town gets when it is in the path of a major storm—it's ours; it's time to do what we've got to do. Corpus Christi had had its share of hurricanes, so getting ready was more of a practiced maneuver than a panicked reaction.

Two of Charlie's maintenance men covered 3140's glass picture windows with plywood while Charlie, at his Driscoll Building office, moved his desk and important papers to the more secure reception area.

Things were jumping at Jones' Lumber and Hardware. Ivory and staff were staying open late for the second day in a row. Hurricanes may be hell for most, but they are heaven for the lumber business.

Ivory loved the wood floors worn down in between the aisles of merchandise. He liked the old oak counters with the glass tops that were scratched opaque. More than that, he loved the wall covered with what he called "shithouse philosophy." A bumper sticker:

> OF ALL THE THINGS I'VE LOST IN LIFE
> I MISS MY MIND THE MOST

was stuck to the wall over a hand-painted sign printed by Ivory's dad who died in 1969:

> REFINISHING AN OLD HOUSE?
> THERE'S NOTHING A LOT OF TIME AND MONEY
> CAN'T FIX
> LOCAL CHECKS ONLY

There were hurricane parties in the young and single apartment complexes. Quite a few drove to San Antonio or Austin to avoid the storm altogether, but most residents of Corpus Christi hunkered down and held on, including the Joneses.

Though invited to stay with Ivory and Evett, everyone agreed it was safe enough to stay in their own home. It was high above the water and solidly built. Charlie's biggest fear was loss of electricity. With windows that didn't open, air conditioning was what made their Ocean Drive home livable.

Closed up, with plywood covering the windows, the normally bright house was like a cave. The only light not being generated by electricity came through the sliding glass bedroom doors. The outdoor louvered door/shutters could be closed at the last minute.

As the winds increased to 35 mph, Jones' Lumber took care of the last customers and closed the storm covers.

One of Evett's storm preparation tasks was to fill the refrigerator with cold Carta Blanca. Over the years they had the hurricane routine down to a science. On the side of his corner-lot house, he had installed a diesel generator as backup power. With a home that didn't need air conditioning, there was more than enough juice to run his appliances and both his neighbors'.

Schools closed. Business shut down. Most everything stopped as the last few hours of waiting began.

Susan tried to do some painting on a canvas and got nowhere. Jeff wanted to get out of the house to cruise but wasn't allowed, so he was stuck in front of a TV that was constantly interrupting with updates and coordinates.

Time took forever until the dark gray clouds began moving swiftly and the wind perceptibly picked up.

HURRICANE GRETA

Category 3

Homes swayed. Glass shattered. Traffic lights were blown from the cables holding them over intersections. At the height of the storm, the palm trees on Ocean Drive looked as though they couldn't possibly survive. Then, as the eye of the storm passed directly over Corpus Christi, an eerie calm that lasted almost 15 minutes overtook the battered city.

Bojangles, cautiously sniffing the air, warily accompanied the trio on their brief tour. Looking downward, they didn't say a word when they saw where the gently sloping cliff had once been. The erosion was short of undermining the foundation of the house and the swimming pool, but it was too close for comfort. As the last light of day gave way to darkness, it was time to get back inside for the second half when the wind would shift directions.

Then the power went out.

The small sounds, the background noises they were used to and didn't notice, all were gone, along with the drone of the TV. There was nothing but silence, the howling of the wind and the driving sound of the rain.

By midnight, things had calmed down enough to venture outside again, so Charlie, Susan, and Jeffrey put on rain gear. The next day when they more carefully surveyed the damage, the sea appeared sweetly docile as small waves gently washed up on a little beach nature had made for herself where the bluff had once been.

The telephones were working by noon. Ivory and Evett had been by early to see how their son, daughter-in-law and grandson had fared. All were impressed by the vengeance and amazed by the damage. The first telephone call they received was from Hal.

"Well, how goes it?"

Charlie told him about the missing bluff and the streets covered with leaves and branches.

"It's about the same here in Robstown, trees and leaves, nothing major. Lots to clean up. I'll drive into town this evening and see how bad your place is. A friend of mine does freelance work with a bulldozer. I've never seen anyone push dirt around as fast as he does. I'll make sure he's available if you need him."

Jones' Lumber and Hardware would be open bright and early the next morning after the storm, with or without power, because there was a generator backup that could run the basics. Since the store still had ceiling fans,

Ivory looked forward to a day with the windows open, the way it was before AC.

Without electricity, it didn't take much convincing to get the Ocean Drive Joneses to move to the Ivory and Evett Joneses where they could get some sleep. Everything worked there and nothing worked at home including the stove—might as well. As Ivory would later point out, at no time did he rub in the fact that there wasn't a cold beer or even an ice cube for a Scotch on the rocks in the fancy big house on Ocean Drive.

For Jeff this was merely more of life's fucking bullshit being dumped right on his head.

Chapter XVII

Rain, Rain, Rain

IT had been raining relentlessly for three days with only brief glimpses of the sun breaking through the tropical depression's fast-moving, low dark clouds. At least the power and air conditioner had come back on so Jeff was slightly less uncomfortable as he sat in the stuffed armchair in his room staring out at the gray of Corpus Christi Bay. The color of the water mirrored the overcast sky as sheets of rain blew across the surface. Slouched down in the feather pillows of the chair as he watched the day's last light fade, Jeff was miserably lonely. Having dumped his skateboard buddies who had been his companions, he didn't have any friends to call or go see.

"Jeff, it's for you," his mother said, knocking on his closed door.

"Jeff, are you okay? Is your house okay?" Lynn asked as Jeff sat upright.

"I guess so, a big part of the bluff washed away."

"You looked so sad last time I saw you at school, and I worried about you during the storm. I called to see if you were alright?"

"Yeah, fine," Jeff responded with resignation overcoming hope.

"Could I come see? I'd like to see what the storm did."

"Why, sure, should I come get you?"

"No, I'll drive over. It's okay isn't it, Jeff, if I come over?"

After assuring her that it was perfectly fine, he jumped out of the chair and rushed to the bathroom to get ready. He smelled of Old Leather aftershave when he walked into the living room to tell his mom that a friend was coming over.

"Don't you look nice," Susan said quizzically.

"Well, Mom, it's this new friend I met, and she wanted to see where the bluff used to be, and I said it was fine." Not knowing what more to say, he fidgeted as he backed up and walked to the front door when he heard a car pull into the drive.

Lynn was smiling as she closed the car door, and Jeff was smiling as he met and walked with her the last few steps to the front door. Susan was smiling as she forced Jeff to introduce her to who she suspected was the mystery blond. There were a lot of even, white teeth smiling and a high level of nervousness as Susan excused herself and went to the kitchen. *Ooh-La-La*, Susan had a little bounce to her step. She couldn't wait to tell Charlie about Miss Cheerleader!

"Wow, so this is it," Lynn said still standing on the marble floor of the entrance hall. Having never been inside, there was a lot to see.

"Yeah," Jeff said with a sheepish grin.

"Well come on, show me," Lynn insisted and took him by the arm.

After the royal tour which included his bedroom and the hidden buzzer, after seeing the bluff erosion and Corpus Christi Bay, Lynn suggested they take the station wagon to see what the storm had done to Mustang Beach and let Bojangles run.

Driving over the same auxiliary road that led to the beach and parking by the same piece of driftwood—bare legs, without shoes in rain jackets—they began walking down the deserted, gray coastline. Bojangles, oblivious to the rain, was happily getting sand in his wet fur. Lynn ran ahead a few yards and threw a piece of driftwood into the surf.

"I missed you, Jeff. Thanks for letting me come over today. I had to get out of the house. Things have been a little claustrophobic."

"I missed you, too much. I shouldn't even tell you how miserable I've been."

Her blond hair was wet and strands were stuck to the side of her face and cheek. Both had pulled the hoods to their jackets back and were ignoring the rain that leaked around the collar and ran underneath. When Jeff put his hand in hers, she stopped and looked up into his dark eyes. When he softly kissed her, Lynn let out a sigh of relief as they wrapped their wet plastic arms around each other.

"Is this happening to me?" Jeff said, as he looked at the raindrops that were trickling down her neck. They found each other's lips again.

"I love you, Lynn," Jeff couldn't help saying it.

"I love you, too."

She was crying as they held each other again for a long time, not saying a word before walking hand in hand back along the water's edge.

The last time she had slept with Todd—the day before the storm—she wanted Jeff. But, if she left Todd for him, there was the very real possibility that Jeff was going to get the holy crap beaten out of him, causing a monumental scene involving pain.

The ride home was subdued as they matter-of-factly talked about the ramifications.

"I was afraid of this," she told him as he turned off the ignition. "I don't know what we're going to do. We've really gotten ourselves in trouble."

"I love you, Lynn, I really do."

"I know you do," she whispered as she reached over and kissed him quickly before opening the door. With a garden hose, he washed the sand off her feet, legs, calves, and knees before she got into her car, waved and drove off.

"Mom, Dad, I'm home," she said in a voice slightly louder than normal. The steaming hot shower felt like heaven after being in the rain. Momentarily blocking out the hornet's nest she'd kicked, she carefully shaved each leg and under each arm.

Cheerleading, doing cartwheels on the sideline, she didn't care about the game. She cared about being in the spotlight as she jumped and her pleated skirt flew into the air. To the thousands of people in the high school stadium, she would scream through her megaphone with "*Lynn*" painted in scarlet on the side, "Who are the Texans?"

Putting her perfectly manicured hand to her ear, the student body would respond, "We are the Texans!!"

"What kind of Texans?"

Looking at a young woman so lively, bright and blond made the fans yell even louder, "The fighting Texans!!!!"

Then, with the audience still watching the field at the end of the game, she would rush up and on tip-toes press herself against her sweaty, grimy football hero whose hand she had to push away from her ass.

Her minor wake-up call had been meeting Jeff that night at the party. He was gorgeous, if unvarnished. Mainly, he seemed like a good guy who didn't strut around like a puffed-up peacock talking about football *all the time.*

Her major wake-up call had been what Todd had said after making love too quickly—something about when they got married. Marriage, what in the fuck was he even thinking about?

I want to be a movie star.

Lynn was damn sure of one thing. She was *not* going to be a Corpus Christi housewife with two cars and two kids married to a beer bellied ex-football player. How shitty-awful that would be for the rest of her whole miserable life.

The subplot, and icing on the cake, was, Jeff's

grandmother had been a real Hollywood actress in real films and was directing plays at the Little Theater—an interesting tidbit she happened to find out about that fit in nicely.

Jeff—she'd have to keep Jeff a secret for a while. They'd have to keep it to themselves until things cooled down. Looking at herself in the steamed mirror, she knew she wouldn't be afraid to do a nude scene. Genetics had been ever so generous with her young, smooth, well-developed, well-proportioned body—blond, blue-gray eyes, perfect teeth, the sexy smile she'd practiced. There didn't seem to be any reason why her dreams couldn't come true if she kept everything out in front of her.

On the other side of the door her mother called out, "Lynn, Todd's on the phone. Want me to have him call back?"

"No, Mom, tell him I'll be right there." No time like the present. She deliberately finished drying herself off and put a fresh towel on her wet hair. In no hurry, she wrapped a white terrycloth robe around her body before she went to the phone.

"Hey, Todd."

"Hi, honey, where have you been?"

"Oh, out with some friends."

"What friends?"

"Nobody," she paused, "Todd, I want to break-up."

Todd thought he'd been sucker punched by a truck.

Without warning he was getting dropped like an H-bomb. Who was it? He begged for her to tell him why, and the only reason she gave him was that she didn't want to be serious anymore. He cried. He said he'd break down the door if she wouldn't tell him face to face.

Not wanting the door broken down, she calmly hung up and said, "Mom, I just broke up with Todd, and he's coming by to beg me not to. I've got to go out with him for a while. Don't worry. I'll be back soon."

Without makeup, hair still wet from the shower, she ran out of the front door when she heard Todd's car pull up. From the living room window, her mother watched as she opened the car door and got in. Tires spinning on the wet cement, off they skidded.

"Good God, be careful," she prayed.

Driving in the rain that was still falling steadily, Todd didn't know how to approach this surprise turn in life. Caught completely off guard, he tried to find out why. He had thought they were happy and that she was in love. No one had ever broken up with him.

He parked in a vacant lot overlooking the bay where he had taken her to neck when they first met. For Lynn, the view was nothing compared to Jeff's, and he had a house with a pool. Jeff's grandmother was an actress.

Repeating how much he loved her, Lynn turned her face to avoid his lips, then pushed hard to stop his hand from moving up her blouse. How could she have fallen in love with this meathead she thought as he kept trying to put his arms around her, trying to make her change her mind. When she opened the door and jumped out of the car, in a moment of rage, he threw the car in reverse and tried to back up and leave.

Unfortunately, neither he nor his tires had a grip on the situation. Black mud flew right up the entire front of Lynn's body and face as the back tires quickly dug in so deeply the car was stuck.

Lynn had to wipe the mud out of her eyes and off her forehead before she could even see what had happened.

There was a lot of yelling before Todd went to knock on the door of a nearby house and ask the elderly lady if he could please call the nearby Texaco Station that would send a truck to pull the car out. Lynn boiled as she pulled clumps of mud from her face, legs and clothes, flicking them to the ground.

Lynn's mom and dad stood gape-mouthed in parental amazement when, three hours later, she stomped through the front door—mud on the front side, clean on the backside—hot shower number three.

News of their breakup traveled quickly. By one o'clock Lynn had been asked out by four guys, two of whom were Todd's friends.

Jeff, the ex-skateboarder, who nobody knew was even in the picture, had to make-do with the wink she gave him as they passed in the hall between classes. This was cool Lynn thought—the drama, the intrigue. There was a plot—and subplot.

Much to his delight, Jeff got the story in detail that night on the phone. Todd, hearing the busy signal every time he tried her number, started calling all the boys he suspected of stabbing him in the back. He didn't know Jeff at all, so he wasn't even a possibility. When he did get through to Lynn, over an hour later, she hung up on him prompting him to try to write her a letter.

With a yellow #2 lead pencil in his big hand, he was having a hard time putting his feelings into words. It was almost midnight when he finally put his heavy heart to bed. Sobbing softly into the pillow, his muscular back shaking, over and over he asked himself, why? Why? What had he done wrong? Since they had been doing the thing husbands and wives do, he was trying to do the right thing. He thought she'd be happy to have him at least mention marriage. Wasn't that what sex was about? Never, ever had he hurt so badly or felt this low and alone.

Chapter XVIII

Life Goes On

DUMP truck after dump truck rumbled down a temporary road off to the side of Charlie's house. All day long there was the incessant downshifting of gears as the trucks slowed to make the turn. Behind the house, there was the hydraulic sound of a truck bed rising to unload as the bulldozer throttled up and down, moving the earth, replacing what "Greta" had taken.

When things were somewhat back to normal, Charlie and Susan had Red, Hal, Ivory and Evett over for a much-needed get-together. It was extra nice by the pool looking out over the calm water after what they'd been through. Everyone had been working too hard.

On an evening this clear, you could see all the way across the bay. When asked, Charlie said that the lights were from a small town called Ingleside.

Evett, the only one of the group who hadn't grown up in Texas— "I've often wondered where the names of these towns came from. Who was Rob? What kind of person was Alice? Falfurrias, Uvalde, Weslaco, Freer—were there bees in Beeville?" These were little towns surrounding Corpus Christi, "Body of Christ," and Laguna Madre, "Mother Lagoon."

I'd better get to the library, Red thought.

Impatient with the small talk, Ivory was dying to ask Hal about the boat.

"Well, Ivory, it's hard to describe exactly what kind she's going to be. I guess that's why we're building it. It will be interesting to see if all these ideas pan out. It's not a sailboat, but it is going to have sails, and I hope it's not too unwieldy with a single screw. Technically, it would be considered a motorsailer.

"Red and I got quite a kick out of the people living on their boats up and down the coast. The sail boaters were the most interesting to talk to, but their boats were generally too cramped for us. After living in a house for as long as we have, we aren't going to be comfortable in something that compact."

"You're going to *live on it*? This is serious."

"The first thing, once I get going, will be the bulkheads, the walls inside the boat." Hal paused, "Ivory, I forgot you were in the Navy."

"Wasn't I."

"I need to cut them out and prop them upside down where they're supposed to go. Then the hull's metal skin can be welded to the frames. It's going to be tricky because the curves are complex if it's going to look like anything at all. I don't want it to look like a box. Two of my men are good at welding. A friend of mine, who's a professional metal man, has promised to keep an eye on what I'm doing to make sure it doesn't fall apart at the seams.

"It's going to be pretty damn big. I want it to be small enough so Red and I can go it alone, but I want it to be large enough so you jokers can come along without bumping into each other every time we turn around.

"Nothing fancy. I don't want the topsides to shine like a new car, and I don't want to varnish a thing above deck. Maybe if I was young I could put on a canvas hat and sit out in the sun doing brightwork, but I'm trying for something in-between.

"The boats I was first attracted to were the crew boats servicing the rigs in the Gulf. I thought they were the greatest things I'd ever seen until I had the chance to ride in one. Rough and noisy as hell. Had to have been designed by oilmen. The philosophy behind them was, put the biggest engines that will fit into the heaviest steel hull that can be built and float. Then cover the whole thing with more steel so no one will get wet, and off you go. They work, but they're like a gorilla."

The storm had been an exhausting experience, but oddly an invigorating one as they talked until late.

Susan felt more inspired than she had for a while. Still teaching some classes, she had relinquished her position as head of the art department. Thinking she would enjoy giving the department direction and cohesion had been noble goals, but the price had been high. Haggling over budgets with the accounting department was dreadful. When Susan finally asked what this bean-counting head of the business school was looking at—he made a point of looking at her ears every time they were in the same room together—he said, puffing on his pipe, he was just making sure they were both there, and then got so tickled with himself tears came out of his eyes as he laughed with his mouth closed.

"Get it? Van Gogh? Ear?"

For him painting would forever be the artsy-fartsy pursuit of some nebulous, intangible that had absolutely nothing to do with the bottom line or the gross national product.

Writers—people can relate to writers much better. Books—you could print a lot of them and sell them and then, if you were lucky, you could sell the rights to a company that had stockholders and make a movie.

Journalism was big, too. Look at fellow Texan Dan Rather.

"Art paintings," were down with the tadpoles. An insurance agent, talking to Susan about home coverage, tried to explain to her how the value of "art paintings" was difficult to establish and how insurance companies were reluctant to pay unless the value of the "art paintings" could be proven.

The painting Susan showed Red wasn't finished but the understated overtone was Mother Nature loves a good storm or a big flood. She enjoys seeing the magnificent rotation of clouds, rain and wind. To Mother Nature, it's like the crashing cymbals of the Corpus Christi Symphony. In winter, a good avalanche in Colorado will do, perhaps an earthquake in Los Angeles or a flood in Missouri.

What especially caught Red's attention was how captivating it is to vicariously feel the strength of a storm in a work of art. On their trip up East, they had seen quite a few paintings of old sailing ships in heavy seas—danger and adventure jumping off the canvas. Red told Susan her new work-in-progress reminded her of the print they had bought on the trip and were having framed—the ship *Cutty Sark* in full sail on rough seas. They thought it would look good opposite the color sketches Susan had used for the Parkdale State Bank mural. Susan was going to throw the three-by-five-foot drawings away, but Red talked her into matting and framing the best ones. They looked perfect in their Robstown home on the wall behind the couch. Red had several "Susans" throughout the house.

The new ingredient to the usual and more frequent get-togethers was the trips to Hal's construction site. It was fascinating to see the progress and listen to Red and Hal talk about what went where and what had been done that week. None of them had ever seen or done anything like this before.

At first, Red thought she would hang around, keep an eye on Hal, and read. She kept a detailed progress journal that not only kept track of the construction, it told the story of those involved. With four extra men around—ready to pour their hearts out to Red or ask for her advice on how to handle some aspect of their lives—there was always plenty in the personal column.

Her role rapidly expanded as Hal bounced different ideas back and forth with her. It wasn't long before she had to give welding a try to see just how hard it really was.

This was an interesting new dynamic. She and Hal had never done any construction together. They had raised kids and made a home, but Red was never that involved in the day-to-day labor of Harlequin rigs.

Charlie and Susan's day worlds were on opposite sides of town. Symbolically, she took a left from the driveway, and he took a right on his way to work. They talked about their days, their frustrations and counseled each other on what to do, but they did their jobs separately.

Evett didn't do much at Jones' Lumber and Hardware these days, but she and Ivory were always involved with Community Theater productions.

A boat can, in the eyes of someone infected with the fever, become a holy endeavor. The grand compromise of comfort versus safety, size versus utility and pocketbook, all intertwined with beauty and function—self-contained with water, fuel, electricity, galley, head and bed. The curves are siren-like in their seductiveness—touching them, running your hands along them, looking at them to see if they are true, is an erotic experience. Hal and Red's boat was a mistress they could both enjoy.

On a beautiful Saturday night in November, Jeff diplomatically declined the invitation to drive out to Laguna Madre Marine and Robstown with his parents.

On that same evening, Lynn kissed her father and

mother's cheeks before she got into her Mustang, "to go with some girls to the movies and later Tri-Drive for a hamburger or something. I'll be home early," she reassured them.

First, she drove to a mall out on Staples, checking her rearview mirror to see if she was being followed. To be sure, she drove a few miles out of town to a farm road that had no traffic and came back into town a different way, taking a left onto Ocean Drive. Looking back one last time to see if Todd or one of his buddies was on her tail, she turned into 3140 Ocean Drive and pulled into the garage Jeff had opened.

With the push of a button, the garage door closed and Jeff led Lynn in through the side door that went from the garage directly to the breakfast room where they stopped and she gave him a big, sweet kiss.

Jeff was floating in someplace as close to heaven as he had ever been. *This was way more than anyone could hope for*. Tasting each other, her lips were cool... then warm...

"Want a beer?" he said looking at her with his hand on her shoulder.

From the breakfast room, they went to the liquor alcove where crystal glassware and liquor bottles were set on glass shelves. Jeff pulled out a couple of Carta Blanca beers from the under-counter refrigerator, cut a lime on a cutting board next to the sink, and squeezed some into each bottle.

Looking around at the stunning elegance after dark, with the recessed lights dimmed, she shook her head and grinned as they meandered through the garden room, where a live rubber tree stood underneath the skylight. Detouring slightly at Susan's corner of the world, he led her through the door to the brick patio by the pool.

Jeff had turned on the pool lights and set the rheostats so the mood would be perfect. From the pool, through the living room picture window, she could see the Steinway B, while across the bay, the lights of town were just beginning to twinkle on the water. The only sound they could hear was radio station KRIS playing the latest hits at a low volume over the outside speakers.

"You like weed?" Jeff asked.

"You've got some? You must still be a boarder at heart," she smiled. *This is going to be great.*

Jeff took a joint out of his pocket and they each took a couple of hits. For a few moments, they quietly looked out at the bay and drank the ice-cold Carta Blanca. Lynn stretched out and put her head on his leg allowing her to look up at Jeff's face and the stars as they began to shine through the nighttime sky. Jeff gently stroked her hair as the "fingernail" moon rose from the east, and day turned to night.

"What should we call ourselves?" Lynn asked mischievously. "Since I've got your ring, maybe we could start a new trend—exchanging earrings."

Jeff had forgotten and felt stupid when she pulled it out of her pocket. It was a pitiful, thin looking thing that Lynn closed her fist around when Jeff reached for it.

"No way buster, it's mine and I'm not letting it get away from me," she said, laughing. Sitting up, she added, "I thought you were crazy the first time I saw you."

"I didn't know what to do, and I was kind of wasted," Jeff said with a shrug of his shoulders. "What are you going to do with it other than make me feel silly?"

"You weren't silly. It was cute, and I'm keeping it forever. No boy has ever given me an earring before."

She was laughing out loud and so was Jeff.

Next Lynn wanted to see Bojangles, so Jeff let him out of the fenced side yard. After he said his hellos, tail wagging full speed, they watched him run to the place where he could wade and look for fish.

When Jeff came back to the patio with their third beer, she wasn't sitting in the chair she had been when he went inside but her shorts, shirt, bra and underwear were. She was hanging on the side of the pool.

"Water's great, come on," she smiled provocatively.

Holy fuck. What do I do?

"I'll get my suit."

"What's the matter, never been skinny dipping?" she said with a cocked head. Though the ripples distorted the water, he could see she didn't have a thing on, *nothing*.

Quickly, uneasily, he pulled off his shirt and jeans trying to cover his immediate embarrassment as he jumped in the water.

"It feels so much better without clothes, doesn't it?" she said in her throaty voice that was lower than one would expect. She was hanging on the side of the pool, in a way he could see her breasts and it made his lungs reflexively suck air.

They spent the next few minutes giggling and holding on to the side of the pool, before she challenged him to a race back and forth, which Jeff barely won in part because he was trying to swim with a hard-on and look at her at the same time. Jeff wanted to put his hands all over her but held off as she dove and swam underwater to the shallow end.

Standing up in water that came to their waists, Lynn looked at how trim Jeff was and how tan he was everywhere except where his bathing suit should have been.

He was more delicate than Todd and far more handsome.

Both in a trance, Jeff put his hands on her waist and pulled her toward him—flesh to flesh, bosom to bosom, man against woman. After a second long, hot kiss with his hands enjoying her wonderful rear end and back, her nipples teasing his chest, Lynn whispered, "Not here," and led him up the pool steps.

Both dripping wet, Jeff opened the sliding door to his room and pulled the down comforter on his bed. They were freezing when they jumped between the sheets and snuggled, laughing, shivering and rubbing each other as they warmed up underneath the covers. Lying on their backs after the first time, breathing heavily, they could see the moon still low on the horizon through the glass door.

Later, after showering in Jeff's marble-walled bathroom, with a towel around her waist, she dried her hair with Susan's hair dryer. Unable to speak over the noise, Jeff could not believe he was looking at this gorgeous half-naked woman, smelling her faint perfume mixed in with the intoxicating smell of the hair dryer's heating element. It was, indeed, a wonderful world.

She waved him a kiss before backing out and putting her car in drive.

By the time Susan and Charlie got home, Jeff had

straightened up the house and was underneath the slightly damp covers looking at the tube. Though he was staring at the television that flickered shadows on the wall, his mind saw only Lynn's naked body. His skin vividly remembered hers.

Driving home with the windows rolled down, Lynn's hair blew carelessly across her cheek as her mind wandered to the purple rush she had gotten when she had been on top, his hands firmly holding her breasts.

Chapter XIX

Muscle & Blood; Skin & Bone

AT first by necessity, Jeff and Lynn pretended to barely know each other though they had become passionate lovers whose seemingly unquenchable lust pulled them together every time they could find a way, even when it was risky.

From the beginning, Susan had a pretty good idea of what was going on behind the scenes. She looked out for them as best she could by concealing any carelessness from Charlie who seemed content to not think about it very much.

Though times had changed, there remained one constant. With children you never know what crisis is coming next.

"Mr. Jones, this is patrolman Harris of the Corpus Christi Police Department. Your son has been involved in an automobile accident. It appears that no one was seriously injured, but your son and his girlfriend are here in the emergency room."

"We'll be right down."

"Mr. Jones, I'll try to wait, but we're short-handed tonight. There are a few things you should know."

"They're okay, Susan. There's been a wreck," Charlie said to Susan, whose face changed from a gray look of, "please let them be all right" to one of sad relief. Tears began running down the colorless cheeks of her face that suddenly showed fatigue in a way that reminded Charlie of how she looked getting into his car at the airport on their way to Monterrey.

"Your son was in possession of alcohol at the time of the accident. His breath smelled of alcohol. I wasn't able to run a sobriety test on him at the time of the accident though he appeared to be mildly intoxicated although he passed the breathalyzer by a fraction here at the hospital. He told us he lost control of the vehicle, a station wagon registered in the name of a Susan Jones, causing it to slip off the side of the road into a ditch on Santa Fe Street near Catalina Place in the Lamar Park subdivision.

No other vehicles were involved in the accident.

"Let me finish, Mr. Jones. The female passenger suffered a cut over the left eye and a chipped tooth. The doctors are checking now for internal injuries and skull fractures. Your son probably has a broken collarbone.

"Mr. Jones, they're going to be all right. I have written up a ticket for minor in possession and for negligent operation of a motor vehicle.

"Yes, sir, Mr. Jones I'll try to be here. Mr. Jones, they were lucky. These are the easy phone calls to make ... Yes, sir. Thank you, Mr. Jones. My best to the Mrs."

Charlie had his pants on by the time he thanked the officer. Susan pulled on a pair of Levis and buttoned her shirt before she brushed her hair, washed her face and brushed her teeth. She hated bras, instead wearing shirts with pockets.

The emergency room, where drama is acted out in real life night after night—anguish, gore, death, and those who are saved. The fluorescent lights and the sparkling, shiny linoleum floors jolted Susan and Charlie when they passed through the sliding glass doors that parted at the direction of an electronic eye mounted over the center of the entrance.

Jeffrey was alone in the waiting room, arm in a sling, looking up at a rerun of *Nick at Night's* "The Partridge Family" on a wall-mounted TV.

Dried blood was all over his pants. He had taken his shirt off so Lynn could hold it over her eye to stop the bleeding.

Lynn's parents arrived about three minutes behind Charlie and Susan.

Jeff, still a little drunk and stoned, clearly did not impress them with his tearful apology. Her parents went straight to the desk and asked about where they could go to see their daughter as Jeff tried to explain how quickly it had happened, pain shooting through his shoulder with every word.

Lynn and Jeffrey's little secret was that the split second came when they dropped a joint of premium Jamaican.

As apologetic as he was, Jeffrey felt he had handled the situation damn well. As much as he hated to, he let the bag of dope sail rapidly downstream with the water in the bottom of the ditch. A lot of blood was running down Lynn's face and hands. Her white blouse was covered with it, and he could see her tooth was chipped so Jeff pulled off his T-shirt and made her hold it to the head wound. She had been thrown against the windshield when the car hit the bottom of the six-foot deep, man-made gully. Irrationally looking for the chipped part of her tooth, he found the roach they'd dropped and ate it. Lynn was still sobbing, breaking his heart, when the police officers arrived.

Tears continued flowing down Lynn's cheeks, and her hands were shaking badly as they wheeled her into the emergency operating room where they would give her four stitches to close the cut above her right eye. He was trying to be supportive, but she was thinking much more about her appearance and the possibility of a scar than she was about holding hands.

If that careless shit screwed up my acting career, I'll kill him.

Hurt, in agony, sitting in the brightly lit waiting room across from his parents and her parents without his shirt on was, without a doubt, the worst and longest hour Jeff had ever endured in his lifetime. They kept wanting to know what had happened. Yes, it was his fault. Yes, they had been drinking beer. No, they hadn't been taking drugs, he lied. It happened so fast. Only a couple of beers. A drive-through liquor store had sold it to them. He must have taken his eyes off the road for a split second. It was an accident. He wasn't drunk. He made a mistake.

Lynn's parents were obviously frightened and angry. Seeing their child covered with blood had shaken them badly.

The orange whirling light of the tow truck was visible from Ocean Drive as Jeff and his dad turned right to see how badly damaged the car was. Blood and the empty beer cans that littered the inside of the car hit Charlie in the stomach like an elbow to the solar plexus.

"You're a lucky boy. You and Lynn could have been killed. You know that, don't you?" was one of the few things Jeffrey remembered from his father's speech on their way home. When they finally did get home, Charlie pulled down a crystal tumbler and filled it with Scotch. Jeff, who couldn't move without searing pain, wanted one too, but he knew that wasn't going to happen.

Jeff's neck and back were tightening up from the collision. The collarbone was so tender he could barely walk. Getting into bed was worse. Susan brought him one of the pain pills that had been given to him at the hospital, hopeful he might get some sleep. She knew she wouldn't.

The ramifications of what had happened to him that night were far from over.

And that was the way he looked at it. Something bad had "happened" to him. He didn't really feel the accident was the result of something he had done wrong. *We all make mistakes.*

The next morning Susan had to help dress him for the orthopedist. Though excruciating, it was nothing compared to what he felt when, after more X-rays, the sling was removed, so he could be fitted with a complicated harness designed to put downward pressure on the fracture. Susan was afraid he might pass out.

When confronted, "You drink, Dad," was Jeff's automatic comeback to Charlie's lectures.

"When you are my age and earn your own living you can drink, too. There *are* a few problems we are going to have to deal with, like 'minor in possession,' for which I'll have to pay a fine. You'll have to serve probation and you'll get to explain this on your college applications and to the judge."

Unable to drive for weeks, missing Lynn, there was pain on all fronts. They talked and she came by every couple of days, which helped, but he couldn't shake the premonition that things weren't the same.

On the home front Jeff pointed out that the wreck hadn't been the end of the world. "Look, Dad, the car is fixed. Insurance paid for everything." Granted, Lynn's stitches had to be redone by a plastic surgeon, but the scar was practically invisible now. The dentist did a great job on the cap—it was impossible to tell.

"Why don't you sue the insurance company," had been Jeff's reply when his father informed him that their rates would be going up.

"Isn't that what you do for a living? It's totally unfair for them to raise the rates just because I had an accident. What was the point of having insurance if they raise your rates every time you make a claim?"

His father just sighed. Normally, he might have argued the point until they were both red in the face, voices raised.

The worst part was that almost everything he wanted in life was going his way before his luck turned and they broke up. He missed seeing the way she crossed her arms to pull her blouse up over her head as she undressed before they made love. He missed her kisses and the way she held on to him in the heat of the night. He missed the drama of sneaking around and finding a time and a place.

God, they were scared the time her parents pulled into the driveway hours before they were due home. He had to hand it to her. She was quick when she had to be. His heart was pounding about a thousand times a minute as he hid, naked, in the back of her clothes closet. He could hear her rushing around before she jumped into the shower as the front door opened.

"Are you home, dear? What's Jeff's car doing outside? Lynn? Lynn? What's going on here?"

"Oh, is that you, Mom? How was your night? Oh, the car? Well, Jeff brought me home. I had the cramps so he dropped me off early. The car? He must have gone with

Nate for a hamburger. I think he said he'd come back for it," she loudly replied over the sound of the running water.

"I feel better now. Nothing like a hot shower. Everything's fine," she reassured her mother as she turned off the water and got out.

"We'll talk tomorrow. Nothing's wrong. I'm just tired."

It was a miracle her mother hadn't seen Jeff's billfold on the floor. It must have slipped out when Lynn kicked his trousers under the bed. She didn't seem to notice the way the bed was rumpled, either. Two hours later, when they finally heard the TV go off in the master bedroom and felt the coast was clear, he crawled out of the window they had used often.

By the time he physically healed, now that he and Lynn were just "friends"—all he did, other than schoolwork, was play golf with some country club brats in the afternoons and sulk.

At the boatyard, Hal and Red were making steady progress as fall turned to winter, before a welcome spring brought back summer. The hull, now that it had been turned upright, looked like a ship at the bow and was rounded at the stern to keep it from looking boxy. One of Hal's better ideas on how to speed up work below deck came to him after he'd noticed how many times everyone was going up and down the ladder.

Boatbuilders wake up in the middle of the night since, even as they sleep, part of their subconscious continues building. After a while, that part of their mind wants the company of the rest of the brain—*Come on Hal, wake up. Atta boy. Open those eyes. You've got work to do.*

Often, usually around three in the morning, Hal would put his hand on Red's side and stare at the ceiling fan going around, mentally working through the next construction challenge.

The fiberglass water and fuel tanks would have to be completely removable because every part of the inside of a steel hull must be accessible.

The size and height of the water and fuel tanks determine how much headroom there will be if the freeboard—the part of the hull that can be seen when the boat is in the water—is to remain aesthetically and nautically pleasant to the eye.

It was during one of these sleepless sessions that Hal came up with the time-saving idea. Filed somewhere in the folds of his gray matter was the memory of an artist's rendition of Noah's Ark. Animals, not being able to climb ladders, entered the boat through a door in the side of the hull.

The next morning, with a torch, Red cut a door-sized hole in the side of their hull making work tremendously easier below deck. They could weld that same piece of metal right back where it had come from and fare in the seam when the time came.

The wheelhouse was constructed on the ground. Having lowered the main engine and both generators onto their mounts, it wouldn't be long until it would be hoisted into place and welded to the deck.

The engine room was going to be fully air-conditioned with stereo speakers mounted in a space large enough to sit down while work was being done. Ivory had successfully argued that music was the only thing that would help keep diesel temper tantrums to a minimum.

During their periodic visits, Susan and Charlie could see the boat taking shape. Looking inside and listening to Red and Hal was an adult version of going to another kid's fort. Romantic images of sailing away from the world and its problems floated freely in everyone's mind, as they looked here and touched there, before getting into their cars for a dinner together. That particular Sunday they drove to the King's Inn in Riviera, a tiny coastal town on the other side of Robstown from Corpus Christi. A good 45-minute drive, the food and atmosphere made the trip worth it.

Inside, the way the wood-frame building had settled over the years caused the floors to slope to one side. Screened in, electric fans kept the air circulating as the waitresses and busboys brought out platters of food and took back empty plates.

Service was family-style with wild game on the menu.

The six of them sat at a large table near the middle in straight back chairs that weren't uncomfortable, but they weren't comfortable enough to linger after dinner. After ravishing the fresh garden tomato and cucumber salad served alongside platters of fried fish, quail, chicken, and the best fried onion rings in the world—tired and ready for bed—they filed out past the cashier as Charlie paid the check. It was his turn.

Right by the door was a stainless-steel toothpick dispenser that delivered them one at a time by rolling the knob on the side. They all took one because it was a long drive back through dark countryside. It was even longer with a piece of food stuck in your teeth.

Red and Hal, in their convertible, drove off first with the rest of the crew not far behind. In the headlights, seeing their silhouette against the night, they could have been teenagers the way she sat next to him—his arm around her—her head tilted back.

Chapter XX

"CHARLIE, I am sorry to wake you up in the middle of the night. I thought I should. Charlie ... he's gone. Hal died about an hour ago."

"Oh no, Red, no," Charlie choked out. Susan immediately took the phone.

"Red, where are you? Is anyone there with you? Hold on honey, we'll be right over."

The Buick was doing over a hundred as they raced down the empty road they had driven so often since Red and Susan met in her life drawing class.

Susan's first reaction had been a practical one because once you have been through something like this you are an expert. Barbiturates were the only way she had made it through that first night and several nights after. Surely, Red's son, the doctor, would be prepared with something.

Their eyes were red and puffy as they numbly went into the house with the lights on at three in the morning. When Red put her arms around them, they held each other for a long while.

"We had all those good years together, and he died in his sleep. I've still got my redheaded boys."

Patrick, the doctor son, his wife and their two-year-old daughter were already there. The youngest was flying in in the morning.

Charlie had to go back out to the car. His emotions were flooding him so badly he needed to cry and talk to Hal without anyone around. As the darkness gave way to the gray of an overcast morning, Red finally accepted sedation and was getting some rest. She would need it. Charlie could barely feel the effects of three big Scotches from the bottle Hal's hands had touched the last time they were over. He wondered how Red was going to live without him, as his throat tightened up again. This is what we all get to look forward to. God damn it, why Hal?

The food started coming around 11 in the morning from friends and neighbors. Someone put a black wreath on the chain-link gates of Harlequin Oil and Gas.

Charlie and Susan, without any sleep other than the few hours before they received the phone call, went to the funeral home, chose the casket and made Hal's final arrangements as per Hal's instructions. Ivory and Evett were crushed when they heard the news. He sat down at his piano and played the songs Hal liked, including "Born to Be a Roughneck," while Evett cooked—both tight-throated, lost in memories.

They drove over later that afternoon with food and a couple of bottles of tequila.

"I wish you could have seen this nervous young cowboy coming on to me inside a honky-tonk outside Cuero," Red said.

"He had on this starched cowboy shirt with sun flowers on it. Smelled like he had been poured out of an Old Spice bottle. I could tell he'd even put it on his chest.

"I knew for a fact he put it on his chest after our first night together at Eddie Brown's Motel. He was full of it, that man, always was. He wanted to make money back then, it was that simple, he wanted it for us and himself. It turned out he knew how in a bigger way than I ever imagined. We both wanted to leave Cuero and Goliad and see more of the world. Before we moved here, he was with those damn rigs more than he was with me."

Red was almost talking to herself at this point.

Everyone was thinking their own thoughts, letting her ramble.

Charlie had Jeff drive Ivory and Evett back to Corpus after Jeff promised he would go straight home and not do anything stupid. He was still having his own troubles with Lynn. Susan felt the weight of the world on her shoulders, as she thought of her poor husband killed by a cabbage truck and Hal and Red. She wanted to go sit on Charlie's lap and put her arms around him and hug him as hard as she could.

Charlie and Susan drove home for the first time since they had arrived, to shower and change before the service that was to be held in the small Baptist church in Robstown. Hal and Red had gone to church with the boys most Sundays. She was comfortable there.

Ivory wasn't comfortable at all. Fuck the young minister with the silver wire-rimmed glasses and the fingernails that looked like they had never had dirt underneath them. It was the lily-white hands that pissed him off as much as anything. Ivory wanted to strangle him. He wished with all his might it was the preacher who was dead instead of Hal. Obnoxious, pious little fuck. Ivory had no aversion whatsoever about telling the Lord how poorly He had fumbled this.

Red held it together as she talked with old friends

of theirs from the oil boom days. She thought about her wedding and the men who were there. With their hats off, she remembered how white the tops of their heads were compared to the tan of their faces. She thought of all the times she had seen the whiteness of Hal's head and his workin' hands at their dinner table by the window overlooking the tomato vines they had planted.

Tomato vines are not particularly picturesque, then again neither was Robstown.

Underneath a mesquite tree, that in the afternoon breeze dropped several pods of its sticky seeds on top of the casket, they lowered Hal and began covering him with dirt—dust to dust; ashes to ashes. Charlie had ordered the tombstone. It would take a week to 10 days to inscribe:

HAL BURTON

1925-1997

Beloved Husband and Father

Oil Man and Boatbuilder

R.I.P.

Patrick, his wife and their little girl stayed at the house for the next few days. The grandchild helped in her own precocious way to relieve the tension. Red's younger son lived in a trailer at Harlequin Oil. He was running the operation these days.

Hal would have been proud of her she thought. He was physically gone, but he was still all over the house, around every corner, in every drawer and on every shelf. She had a lot of long conversations with him. She would for the rest of her life.

After Red had been alone for two days, Susan drove over and wouldn't take "no" for an answer when she insisted Red come to town with her. Charlie needed to talk to her about some things, and Susan couldn't stand the thought of Red staying another night by herself. That evening, they ate at Mac's where there was comfort in the lively restaurant noise and the jukebox.

"He sure liked you and Charlie. He was proud of getting the boys through college, but he never regretted not going himself. He told me about his first day on the job and how awkward he felt in his brand-new aluminum hard hat and never-been-washed gray coveralls that zipped up the front. He knew after his first shift that he was doing what he wanted to do.

"He could laugh. I think some of his biggest laughs were on him and how far he had come from his days in Cuero. He'd come all the way to Robstown. If that isn't moving up in the world!"

When they got back to 3140, Charlie asked Red if

she would come to the office the next day, so he could show her how they had set things up. He went to bed while Susan and Red stayed up past midnight, reminiscing and laughing occasionally.

Red knew it was going to be hard. Still, she didn't know it was going to be this hard.

"Thanks Susan," she said the next morning as she headed to Charlie's office.

The next two weeks took forever. While time was standing around, they still had to go to work, cook their meals, go to school—the things that had to be done every day. Susan and Red talked on the phone sometimes for a half an hour, sometimes an hour.

Friday afternoon on a whim, Charlie drove to the boatyard after an uninspiring day at the office and was surprised to see Red's convertible parked beside the trailer and park bench. There was a towel across the back seat so her bird dog, Jim, wouldn't get boatyard dirt on the seats.

The sky was turning black toward the north. Finally, another winter was on its way. Red, sitting on the bench with her knees pulled up to her chest, was watching the dog run with his nose to the ground—probably looking for Hal.

Charlie parked the car and walked over.

"I didn't think I'd see you here. I'll go if you want."

"No, Charlie, have a seat, there's beer in the trailer if you'd like one."

After being neglected for only three weeks, the topsides were beginning to show rust. It reminded Red of an orphaned child stoically wondering who her new parents would be. On the day Hal died, there had been activity—power tools and welding torches. Since then, rain had erased the footprints. The boys had cleaned up the site, put everything up in the shed, and locked it.

Charlie couldn't help but think how lonely Red must be and how beautiful she was.

"What are you going to do?"

"I don't know. I'm thinking about taking a trip for a week or two by myself. Susan told me she was in bad shape when you took her to México. It makes sense, what she told me, that is.

"She said that everywhere in Corpus Christi, gloom and doom had followed her, but when she got to Monterrey, no one knew her or knew they were supposed to feel sorry for her. She could act like a normal person again. People spoke in their normal tones, and she could smile a regular smile. There wasn't a memory around every corner.

"Susan told me I'm going to have to live through the hurt and it never goes away, but she said it felt good to act like herself for the first time.

"I'm sure you wonder what in the world Susan and I talk about on the phone for hours."

A gust of wind made a "dust-bowl" swirl between them and the boat.

"You're going to like this, Charlie, when we named Hal's oil company Harlequin Oil we didn't even know what a harlequin was—only that it was the name of those romantic novels I was reading to pass the time while he was gone. We didn't even think to look it up in a dictionary, if we even had one at the time. I guess we thought it was a last name—Mr. Harlequin.

"Then we were at a cocktail party several years ago when this lady—a nice lady—asked why we would name an oil company after a comic character that wears a mask, has pointed glasses and slanted eyes, wearing checkered, gay-spangled tights ... Boy, you talk about getting caught off guard. With what I'm sure was a bewildered smile, all I could think of to say was that it was a long time ago—and excuse myself by asking where the lady's room was.

"Then I hurried home and told Hal who froze for a second, half-laughed and then laughed out loud. His own oil company was named after a character wearing 'checkered, gay-spangled tights—a clown.'

"This was a big deal for us, digesting the fact that

everyone who knew what a harlequin was must have thought we were goofy, clever, weird, or who knows what?

"Hal decided it fit."

There was something Harlequinesque about poking holes in the ground, as much on a hunch as anything else, to find this filthy black gold that would explode inside the steel cylinders of these cars we drive around."

The cold front was almost on them making Red speak more loudly as they got up, "We both agreed there was something comical about the two of us ducks—I told you about the harlequin ducks, didn't I—out here in the middle of nowhere, building a boat?"

The rain was about 100 yards from them when, just before getting into their cars, Charlie and Red hesitated so she could finish her thought. Looking into each other's eyes, "Nothing but *Harlequin* sounded right." Smiling a little downward smile, "Hal cut the steel letters himself. They're in the shed."

Little poofs of dust jumped up around the large drops as they began hitting the dry dirt. Charlie helped Red with the top, and she rolled up the windows before letting Jim jump in the back seat, getting mud all over the towel.

"Follow me home, Red."

"No, I'm fine, Charlie, really I am," she said over

the thunder as she got inside her car.

"Okay, I'll meet you there," she relented.

What in the world were they going to do with it now? Charlie walked up the ramp built like Noah's Ark and went into the belly of the steel hull. Inside the main cabin, there was a bare light bulb hanging from an extension cord, which he turned on as he sat on what Hal had informed him was a "settee." After a while, he walked forward to the three bedrooms, accidentally ripping the pocket of his suit pants on a metal corner.

Taking in as much as he could, Charlie guessed a double bed or something close could fit in the small cabins. He looked in where Hal said the heads were going to be—one on each side.

The rain had almost quit and the sky had lightened up by the time he emerged, damp and dirty. The blue leading edge of the norther was moving southeast, probably over his house about now.

Chapter XXI

Get Away

ARRIVING at Albuquerque's Southwestern-styled airport, Red walked down a concourse decorated with Native American art, picked up her luggage and went directly to the rented Chevrolet Impala. From the airport she drove east on Interstate 40 turning off on New Mexico State Road 14 called the Turquoise Trail—the slower, scenic route to Santa Fe.

Along the way there were purple mountains, mesas flat as table tops, cactus alongside the gullies washed out from winter's melted snow and *Goddamnit* to fucking hell she wished Hal were with her. Red pulled over to the side of the road where she began beating the steering wheel while she screamed until she slumped over, shaking. She was alone. Her husband, Hal, was gone.

Low gray clouds were forming as she drove through the old gold rush towns of Golden, Madrid, and Cerrillos and saw the vista at Sandía Crest. Temperature in the 40's, it was dropping as the sun silhouetted far-off mountains against a gloomy sky.

It was dark when she pulled into The Bishop's Lodge. Cordial, the woman wearing a bolo tie took her information and summoned a young man in jeans and cowboy boots to show Red to one of the newer Southwestern-styled rooms that had a spacious living area and fireplace.

After freshening up, she walked back to the Lodge for a double tequila at the bar before going to the dining room where she ordered a filet mignon and a bottle of Saint Émilion. The few guests who were there—it was a slow time of year—couldn't help but notice the somber, attractive, older woman sitting by herself seemingly oblivious to her surroundings.

Afterwards, from the window in her room, Red saw the first snowflakes of the year coming out of darkness into the outdoor lights as she lit the bundle of tinder underneath the firewood.

When the bottle of wine was gone, she put a blanket over herself and fell asleep on the couch in the glow of the embers.

The sun was out when Red awoke to unfamiliar surroundings. Anxious, she skipped breakfast and drove to the town square. For starters, she had a local favorite—a bag of Fritos cut open and covered with chili from the Woolworth's Five-and-Dime. Then in the cool, fresh, clean air she began browsing bookstores, especially those with vintage books on the Old West and the Santa Fe Trail.

It was nights in front of the fire that were so sad all she did was drink knowing she would never again see Hal's smile or feel him next to her in bed—that was the worst.

Four long days later, Red was so anxious to see Susan, she arrived at the Albuquerque airport over an hour early to pick her up.

In the glow of twilight, they went to the outdoor patio next to the Lodge's dining room and started with a margarita. Sitting next to the adobe fireplace, they had a lot to talk about and catch up on.

"Did I tell you that Santa Fe was where I told my parents I was going when Charlie picked me up at the airport for our secret trip to Monterrey? I was going crazy in Corpus."

Susan told Red about Charlie in high school and the time she rescued him from the morning-after at church.

She told her how that Sunday morning eventually led to their bedroom scientific sex rendezvous, which made Red laugh, "How in the world did you get the nerve?"

"Lord, I don't know. My brains were in my underwear."

"Trust me Susan, I *know* horny."

"Red, I'll be the first to say that I was envious of the way you and Hal were doing something together. I guess it was meant to be that Charlie and I go our own way and then meet back in the middle. If we can get Jeff off to college without killing himself, maybe we can take some time to catch up with each other. God, I was hoping Hal would make it longer, about 20 years longer."

"Me, too...."

At home in Corpus Christi, Charlie and Jeff were surviving. Angie, the housekeeper, made sure there was good Mexican food in the refrigerator that they could heat up. For the first time in years, they played golf together. Jeff, who had taken lessons as a youngster, could hit the ball a country mile with a country club swing. Where Charlie was hitting a five iron to the green, Jeff was hitting a nine iron or wedge. In between shots, they talked about college and what Jeff saw in his future. His grades were good enough, and he had managed to keep them up despite his love traumas.

Charlie could tell Jeff, with his on-again off-again relationship with Lynn, was dealing with heartache. He also noticed Jeff's new white FootJoy golf shoes, and how Jeff's clubs glistened in the large leather, expensive-looking golf bag. As a matter of fact, his son looked a little too good. Jeff dressed like the pro-golfers who walked the country club fairways in-between Dean Witter and Cadillac ads.

Meanwhile, Jeff was making an effort to get along and even tried to give ol' Pop some golf tips. "Dad, you have to feel good about yourself to play good golf. Read the magazines. It's mental. Visualize your shots. There are lots of players with good swings. When I look at a green, I divide it into quarters like a pie and then decide which quarter I want my shot to land in. If I feel right, have confidence in my swing and my shot-making ability, I can make the ball go where I want it to go."

Jeff reminded his dad that football player Jerry Rice of the 49ers felt he had to look his best to play his best.

Charlie wasn't ready for Jeff to go back to his skateboard, but he wasn't ready for this Jeff, either. Was this the person Charlie wanted to send out into the world —ready to take on life with a new PING putter and a blond cheerleader?

When Charlie agreed to let Jeffrey take it easy the summer before, he envisioned a Norman Rockwell character, walking the course, carrying used clubs, wearing worn brown leather shoes. This was not what Charlie saw as they bounced along in the E-Z-GO electric cart.

There's nothing wrong with what Jeff's doing, Charlie kept telling himself. There is nothing wrong with wanting to dress well and look sharp. Golf is something he will be able to use in making business connections, and that is a lot more important than learning how to deliver lumber in a purple Jones' Lumber truck as his dad had suggested— "Suit yourselves, boys, the offer's there—a day's work didn't hurt you, Charlie."

Because Charlie was the first in his family ever to be a member of a country club—the CCCC, Corpus Christi Country Club—Charlie took up golf late in life and didn't have time away from the office to practice much. He was always going to have a quick swing. Unlike Jeff, the country club swagger and pro-shop lingo were never going to be second nature to him.

In Santa Fe, after a sojourn downtown and a meal at The Lodge, Susan and Red settled in front of the fire in their room and once again began trying to sort out the meaning of life. When the bottle of wine was gone, Red pulled out a bottle of Sauza Herradura and cut up some limes. It was close to midnight when she told Susan of her grand notion.

The next morning, Susan awoke with a raging headache and a mouth so dry she could barely swallow. Looking in the mirror, her eyes were bloodshot, her skin was pale and her lips were cracked from the dry air. Pulling off her nightshirt, she robotically turned on the faucet—a steaming hot shower was a start. As the water pelted the base of her skull, it all started coming back to her. She was pretty sure she was in major trouble.

Egged on by the glow of 100% agave, this is how Red had introduced her bright idea:

"Susan, let me run this by you. Now, keep an open mind and don't get carried away with logic. To begin with, I am already bored to tears. I need to do something to keep my hands and mind busy. I may not look it, but I feel young, too young to shrivel up and call it quits. Paying a gigolo to escort me to Monaco sounds almost dreadful.

"A gigolo might not be too bad, Red. The problem is, they're going to open their mouths and try to make conversation."

"What a shame....

"Susan, listen to me." After even more talk about the meaning of life, after an intense, perhaps insecure, pause, she slowly said, "I want to finish the *Harlequin*." A little more rapidly she continued, "It makes sense financially. If we sell her now, we'll get half of what she's going to be worth finished. I want to do it for Hal, and I want to do it for myself. I am going to need help along the way, but I'm sure I can do it. If I get two of the four men back who were working on it, we won't go as fast, but so what? I've got the next step covered, lifting the wheelhouse on the deck and welding it into place."

Reaching for the bottle and pouring themselves another shot, Red reiterated, "I know I can do it," as she began reciting parts of conversations she had had with Hal.

"A boat is a curious thing. Looking at the whole, building one can scare the pants off you. But, if each little thing is looked at as a single project, the whole isn't quite so overwhelming. I'll have to study Hal's plans more than I did before, but I'm sure he has drawn out the answers to most everything.

"When we were working together, he conceptualized and explained how to do what he wanted us to do. He had everything planned out, and he drew it to scale. There must be 50 drawings," Red said looking at Susan with a tear in her eye. "I've got nothing to lose."

What surprised Susan was not Red's idea to finish the *Harlequin*. No, what surprised her was that she hadn't figured out what Red had been up to. Of course, Susan wanted to be a part of it. She heard the Siren's Song, and her mind started going a million miles a minute. Two women boatbuilders—it sent cold chills up and down Susan's spine—the thrill of it all. They toasted each other with another generous shot.

Standing in the shower, her sober thoughts were: "What in the shit am I doing? What in the hell am I going to tell Charlie? This is nuts. What on God's earth have I gotten myself into?"

Susan also remembered saying, "Red, that is the most wonderful idea, as long as I get to do it with you. If we do it together, we ought to be able to figure it out. I know we can. Think we should fly back tonight and get started tomorrow?"

Oh, boy.

"I was hoping you'd help me," Red had said quietly as though a prayer had been answered.

"I wasn't sure whether you'd want to or not. I'll tell you up front, it's going to be a lot of hard work. I was willing to go it alone. I really was ... partner."

Susan was holding a towel over herself when Red came back from the breakfast buffet with a plate of fresh fruit, eggs, bacon, and sausage.

"I figured this might take a little hair off the dog."

Susan, her wet uncombed hair dripping on her

slumped shoulders, feeling awful, "You were serious, weren't you?"

Red, walked over and softly patted Susan's arm, "We have our work cut out for us. Get dressed. We've got a lot to talk about and I want to go to Shidoni Foundry to see the outdoor metal sculpture. From what I've heard, I'm going to need some green chili chicken enchiladas at the Pink Adobe this afternoon.

Susan feeling fragile, gingerly sat down in front of the plate of food and put a piece of crisp bacon in her mouth. It tasted good.

In the car and later over lunch and margaritas, Red went on, "I've got the wheelhouse covered. You can help me get it in place and that will teach you a lot. The biggest lesson Hal and I learned was to have some fun with this thing. There's no screw-up that can't be fixed. One of our running questions was, 'What's the worst that can happen'? Promise me you won't cut off any fingers. We can go at our own pace, but there will come a time when we'll be over it and ready to move on to something else. It's dirty and it's sweaty, yet there's something good about getting hot and tired. It beats the hell out of worrying about your fingernails."

"Do you really think we can do it?" Susan was margarita numb and hungover—shocked at the idea and the role she had apparently agreed to.

"Susan, I do. I know we can."

With salt on her upper lip and the perfect amount of hot on her tongue—maybe, just maybe, but they would need help.

Red and Susan were going to have to spend a lot of time studying Hal's drawings and reading the books he accumulated. Also, there was a garage filled with parts he had ordered through Ivory using Jones' Lumber to get a discount. It was going to be a big job just finding out what went where.

One of their first goals, they decided, would be to get Ivory on board. If Ivory or someone he recommended could get going on the woodwork below deck, that would be a load off Red's shoulders.

On the flight back to Corpus Christi they began making lists and as they did, it dawned on Susan that Red was in the embryonic stages of rejoining the living in ways not dissimilar to the moment she had the courage to call Charlie, make him take her out to dinner and then go with him to México.

It also became crystal clear that helping Red build this boat was something she should do. Turning her head toward the window, looking down at farmland, even more tears began rolling down her cheeks.

Red then hit her with a shocker, "The other thing I have been thinking about is wiring and motors. I know what Hal had in mind, in theory. I can probably figure out how to do most of it, and we can hire a mechanic, but, and I know you are going to laugh, but I know the right man for the job, and I think I know who his helper should be."

"Who?"

"Charlie, Susan, Charlie's the one."

She smiled and laughed once. "Charlie? My Charlie?"

"Yep, and I'll tell you why. One, if we do this without him, he is going to feel left out, jealous, and become difficult. I am not going to ruin your marriage. Can you imagine, assuming the others' help, how he would feel with everyone except him involved?

"Two, I think Charlie is in a bit of a rut himself though he certainly wouldn't admit it. That's a hunch. You know better than me.

"Three, the night we had dinner at your place, after he and I ran into each other at the boatyard, I dropped Jim off and drove straight over. You and I had been talking for at least 45 minutes before Charlie drove up. You wondered how he had gotten so wet and dirty and how he had ripped the pocket of his suit pants.

"He went inside and looked around the *Harlequin*.

Susan, he was late. He was dirty. I think we can sign him."

Chapter XXII

Implementing the Plan

"WELL, I'm glad you and Jeff got along while I was gone," Susan told Charlie. "It did you good to spend a little time together. I could see it at the dinner table." Later that evening in bed, Susan and Charlie had a chance to really talk for the first time since her return.

"Susan, did you know he charged a new set of golf clubs at the pro shop last month and that he buys a new sleeve of Titleist balls every time he plays? He claims even the slightest scuff mark messes up the aerodynamics of the shot.

"'Dad, wouldn't it make you mad if you hit the perfect shot and it faded off to one side because there was a rough spot on the ball?' is how he put it."

"Charlie, I have no idea what goes on at the golf course. That's your department. You're the golfer. What's the matter with having new balls? Personally, I like the old balls just fine, but you know me, old station wagons—same old man, same old balls."

"It's not the money, so what is it? Why am I feeling guilty about spoiling our child? He's a nice kid. He's got his problems; don't we all? His grades are okay. He'll go to college, go to work, earn enough money to keep him in new clubs and balls, have a family and everything will be as it was meant to be. Now, why do I feel like I'm cheating him? Why do I feel he's missing something?"

"Haven't we had this discussion in reverse a few times? I agree, make him use old balls. That'll teach him something about hardship."

"My, aren't we smug after our little vacation in the mountains? I've been worrying about you and hoping you and Red were okay and worrying about Jeffrey. Then you come back with a devil-may-care grin. I have seen this side of you before and I'm worried."

"I have a plan, Charlie Jones," Susan said, as she started fooling around with her man's real Achilles' heel located about a yard up from his feet. After running her tongue lightly over his old balls until his toes curled and his entire body went rigid from the sensation, she moved up to kiss him and begin a ride that had her moaning and laughing at the same time.

After she rolled off and they caught their breath, Susan said matter-of-factly, "Charlie, I'm going to help Red finish the *Harlequin*, and we want you and Jeffrey to help us. I'm sure Evett will join us. It's going to be like Dolly Parton, Emmylou Harris and Linda Ronstadt's harmonies. We can do it. You've got to help us, though. We need your help. You're in charge of the engines, wiring, and electronics."

Propping himself up on one elbow, "What are you talking about?

"I don't know anything about motors and wiring. I'm an attorney. You don't know anything about boats, either. What is this?"

"Charlie, you're a man, and men instinctively know about engines and RPMs and horsepower the same way women know how to sew. A woman who's never had a needle in her hands can still sew on a button because she consciously or subconsciously takes note of how it's done. It's the same way with you men and motors. You generally know what the parts are underneath the hood of the car. You know about plugs and where they're pointed."

"Susan, marine diesel engines don't even have

plugs and points, they have injectors."

"See that's what I mean, you know these things."

Then, Susan came in with a knockout punch. She delivered the blow with such force and timing there was no way Charlie could deflect it.

"Charlie, we owe it to Hal and to everyone who has dreams and tries to make those dreams come true." Coming back with the left hook, "We owe it to Jeffrey who's going to have a new summer job."

Off guard, flabbergasted, Charlie was at a complete loss. He didn't know what to say.

"Hal's got everything drawn out, where the fuel filters go, everything. You can figure it out. The one thing I promise you—if it's not something you can handle, you are free to bail out like a lily-livered coward, walk off and leave us poor women all alone to do the work because somehow, we *will* get it done.

Oh boy. "Who's going to pay for all of this?"

"Red, but who cares Charlie, we'll work it out. Jeffrey won't be needing all those new balls, and he won't be wearing out his shoes and golf clubs.

"Charlie, if you're good, we might let you be vice-honorary captain or something like that."

"Susan, I am a sought-after, working attorney with international clients. We can hire a mechanic, that shouldn't be a problem."

"No, Charlie, that's not the point. We want you. I love you. *You* saved my life."

On the phone the next day to Susan, "How'd it go?"

"I laid it on him real hard. I'm sure it's just beginning to sink in."

Red smiled, and then added, "I'm coming into town this afternoon to drop off some drawings and books that Charlie'll need. They're all done in Hal's own handwriting."

Leaving the office that afternoon, Charlie took off his jacket and placed it neatly over the back of the passenger side along with his tie, the way he always did and headed for home, but at the last minute, instead of pulling into the driveway, he kept driving until he got to Mac's Restaurant.

Choosing the same corner booth he'd shared with Susan, he ordered a Shiner beer and, instead of Scotch, a shot of tequila neat with salt and lime. In the miniature jukebox mounted on the wall between the Naugahyde overstuffed seats, he put in a quarter and punched A-11, Los Lobos, "Will the Wolf Survive?" as tears ran down his face.

After some deep breaths that he blew out through his mouth like an athlete to gain composure, he wiped the tears from his face with the cold wet napkin that had been under his frosted mug, tossed back the tequila that burned on the way down and took a couple of long pulls on the cold draft beer. Leaving a $20 tip, Charlie walked to the cashier and paid the check.

Earlier that afternoon, Red had come by Susan's carrying the drawings made by her late husband's hands. In pencil, were detailed sketches of the fuel tanks, the fuel line dimensions, fuel filter placement, exhaust and muffler arrangement. Everything was drawn carefully to scale.

Seeing the drawings for the first time had been so hard on Susan, she had to go wash her face, dry her eyes and breathe deeply before she could rejoin Red, who put her arm around her shoulder.

"It is very strange that Hal went to the trouble to draw things out as carefully as he did. I know he enjoyed drawing to scale with his black triangle rule.

"But, I have to believe he made the drawings for us —in case. I don't think we could do this if he weren't still here in his own way to guide us."

There were articles clipped from boating magazines on marine exhaust systems and generators with the important paragraphs neatly underlined. They were in folders organized and labeled along with books on marine wiring, etc.

Before they left, Susan wrote Charlie a note that she put beside the folders and plans: "We're at Ivory's. I should be home around six. I Love You, Susan."

Of course, Ivory agreed—so did Evett, which didn't surprise Susan at all. They'd been helping Hal and Red all along by using Jones' Lumber and Hardware to order marine products wholesale. Ivory thought he and Evett would look pretty damn good on a yacht in a secluded lagoon near some exotic island.

Ivory, before Hal's death, had been trying to locate a good source of teak to use below deck. Resistant to dry rot, it was a beautiful and easy wood to work if you used carbide blades. The new epoxies worked well and were a lot easier to mix than the deep red-colored Resorcinol glue, although the latter was probably stronger.

"I've got the man, Bob Gomez," Ivory said right off the bat.

"Hal and I had talked about using him. He's a good cabinetmaker, fair when it comes to money, and he's a hell of a nice guy. We can fabricate quite a bit at his shop, and do the rest at the boatyard. My table saw and bandsaw are gathering rust in the garage. There's a table sander at the lumberyard no one is using.

"I can get a shipment of teak down from Houston in a week, which we might as well do. Bob's got a planer we can run it through."

They talked about thickness and where the wood should be used. It was obvious from the conversation that Ivory and Hal had gone over this aspect of the construction at length.

Susan and Red didn't think they should leave Charlie alone for too long, so they went back home to see his reaction to the plans Red had brought over earlier.

On the six-sided walnut and marble table in the garden room, underneath a light that hung down from the 24-foot ceiling, were technically and dimensionally detailed drawings done with a draftsman's precision.

With Jeff looking over his shoulder, Charlie was studying them.

"This is cool, Dad."

A half hour later when Susan and Red came in through the side door—the rest of the room was dark except for the plans laid on the table—they looked at each other and then at Charlie with eyes open a little wider than normal.

"You're really going through with this, aren't you?"

They nodded, "Yes."

"Do you know, Hal gave the dimensions of every brass hose fitting that goes on the fuel lines ... Susan, Red, this is insane, it's nuts, aren't you scared?" They both nodded in unison, neither looking very brave.

Jeff, unaware of what was going on, was looking back and forth.

After a pause, "Shit, I'm in," he said and watched their shoulders drop and their lungs exhale. Susan hugged him hard before looking up at his bemused, resigned smiling face. Never in all their time together had she been as proud of him as she was at that very moment. *My Charlie.*

The next day, sitting behind his desk at the office, Charlie thought about the commitment he'd made. He had a good idea what was going to be involved and a little voice within kept whispering,

This is a good thing, Charlie, a very good thing.

Playing golf with the same men every weekend, saying the same things, shooting about the same score—sometimes a little better, sometimes a little worse, but about the same, hadn't been all that much fun these days. Lately, work had been routine. Hal's death had taken a lot out of everyone, and though he knew what they were about to do would be tough emotionally, maybe it would help.

He could already hear the conversations, "Well, my wife and this friend of hers, Red Burton, talked me into helping them with a boat idea they have. Crazy really."

"Is that the boat Hal, the fella' who died recently,

was building?"

"The same."

"What'cha going to do with it."

"I don't know. Red and Hal had been doing the building themselves, now Susan and Red think they can finish the work."

"Who are they going to get to do the job, I mean, who even does work like that?"

"That's the problem. Mom and Dad are helping. It looks like I am, too. So's Jeff."

"You ever worked on boats before?"

Actual work officially started when they began going through the boxes in Hal and Red's garage. The Edson wheel was bronze with teak handles and a teak rim circling the outside of the handles. The compass was a big, brass Danforth Constellation with ornate compass points. Rather than use commercial "dead lights" to bring natural light below deck, there were four "tragaluz"—donated by Ivory from one of his expeditions to San Miguel de Allende, México. They were one-inch-thick and one-foot-square pieces of glass with prisms molded into the underside. In México they were used in houses.

Inside large boxes stacked on top of each other were two "Marine Air" air conditioners, a big bronze propeller, seven 1 ½-inch Thru-Hull fittings and 12 opening portholes. Off to the side were the manual Wilcox Crittenden "Skipper" heads and the accompanying waste treatment systems. On a shelf were polished bronze hand pumps made in Australia for pumping fresh water into the galley and heads. Compared to the electric pump and plumbing complexities of a hot-and-cold water pressure system, the hand pumps were, for Hal, a simple water-saving solution.

Interior light fixtures, not yet out of their sealed cellophane boxes, were close by a spool of number 12 duplex marine copper electrical wire. The bronze running lights were the best money could buy. Nothing but the best and the brassiest for the *Harlequin*.

Charlie took inventory on a clipboard and compared it with the invoices to make sure they weren't overlooking anything.

Next, was to collectively visit the *Harlequin* herself. Almost three months had passed since any work had been done, and the neglect showed. Rust was bleeding down her sides, changing the color from silver/black to reddish brown. Water stood in the bottom of the hull, breeding mosquitoes underneath the temporary plywood cabin floor.

Dumbfounded and more than a little overwhelmed by the enormity of what they were about to do, everyone was in need of comic relief, and Charlie unconsciously supplied it with his "work clothes." The funkiest he could come up with was a pressed khaki shirt, khaki pants and tennis shoes. Everyone else had on faded jeans, old shoes and worn shirts. "Fuck 'em," he'd paid for most of his college education playing football in the mud and blood. Let them laugh, he'd get dirty soon enough.

And Charlie, in his inimitable way, was the first to get to work. He took his new Stanley rule from his belt and headed for the engine room. Carrying a black plastic notebook with a fresh legal pad, he started making measurements and writing notes to himself.

"The 'to-do' lists" would become a joke, as they seemed to get longer. Everyone had their own, but it was Charlie who started titling his list with ridiculous numbers like, "List Number 4,281." That's how they all felt.

It was up to Red to make final decisions, but it was with everyone's input, including two former roughnecks that were handling the metal work and doing a lot of the welding.

Along with the emotional baggage the *Harlequin* carried, there were sequence problems and general confusion. But, step by step, as they started getting into a better rhythm, they began to understand how brilliantly thought out the *Harlequin* was. The deck layout was the epitome of rational simplicity. From midship forward, it was flush. Aft of midship, there was a raised cabin about the area of a king-sized bed. Attached to and aft of the raised cabin was the wheelhouse whose floor was up eight inches from the deck. The raised cabin sole in the wheelhouse improved visibility and allowed for opening ports above the engine room so the hot air could rise and escape.

The engine room was exactly what one would expect from an oilman. It had standing headroom, and there were strategic places to sit that would facilitate dirty work like oil changes.

Almost daily they would come upon something Hal had designed and say to themselves, "Okay, I see what you're doing, Hal." For 20-some-odd years, Hal had worked on every little thing, every minute detail.

If a bunch of steel, sawdust, mess and paint could be poetic, the *Harlequin* was Laguna Madre's *Walden Pond*.

Chapter XXIII

Rhythm and Dues

BY the time Ivory finished the tank molds, Charlie and Susan had primed and painted the engine room. Having read the articles Hal had clipped out and a "how-to" book on fiberglass, Charlie was ready.

There is nothing quite like the very first time a person catalyzes a bucket of polyester resin. The urgency to use it before it hardens triggers a little panic button, no matter how elaborate the preparation.

First, using a throw-away brush, he painted the mold made from plywood with the thick resin. Next, Charlie put pieces of fiberglass mat (random strands of glass) on top of the painted surface and saturated them with resin. Within minutes, Charlie had strands of glass fiber all over his hands and the paint brush. Everything was sticking to everything as Charlie tried to pull the strands from one hand only to have them stick to the other. While this was going on he unconsciously scratched his head, leaving some there.

Boatbuilding is not the dull type of work a person might expect. It is exciting in its own strange way. Getting the parts for a specific project shaped and ready for assembly is the foreplay. The final act of putting them together while the glue is "working" is the drama that leads to the climax and moment of creation.

As winter turned to spring, Charlie was clearing his desk for summer so he could devote his full effort to the *Harlequin*.

The change in his life—this sabbatical—was "interesting." He had seen client's eyes glaze over as he went into lawyerly talk. The same thing was happening when Charlie tried to relate the fascinating progress they were making at the boatyard. The uptown professionals and workday associates he spent time with, tuned out whenever he brought up the subject.

Harlequin-wise, a visual milestone came when the completed wheelhouse was lifted into place. Everybody helped as the entire steel structure that had been fabricated on the ground was slowly lowered, with some cajoling as it dangled from the travel lift onto the deck where it would be permanently welded.

Aesthetically, the *Harlequin's* lines were, at that very moment, defined. Over and over, they admired the results and complimented Red on how beautiful she looked. If only Hal could have been there. But he spiritually was, and his presence was felt every single day and every single time the plans showed them what to do.

Perhaps the greatest thing about Hal's design was its attitude. Not wanting to build a spiffy yacht, he envisioned a boat that would be at home tied up with the oil rig boats and tugboats in Harvey, Louisiana, yet would oddly fit in at a yacht club or public marina.

Ivory and Bob were doing some fine woodwork below deck. Unlike the others, they knew what they were doing. If Hal's plans said, "build a table with a folding leaf: four-foot, two-inches by four-foot, three-inches," that's what they did. The large table that folded on one side was a work of art.

Ivory had done a fair amount of house carpentry, but never anything as precise or demanding as what he was doing on the *Harlequin*. Doors, drawers, bookshelves, teak trim, gratings for the showers, a beautiful teak cabin floor—Ivory was into it with a vengeance.

He was also in charge of the music played on the shed stereo. Everyone could bring their favorites, and Ivory wasn't obnoxious about it. He was open to all types. He merely filled in the gaps between the radio and tapes others wanted to hear. The number of hours they were putting in left plenty of time for tunes. Among the occasional favorites was Jimmy Buffett's "Migration":

> And that's why it's still a mystery to me
> Why some people live like they do
> There's so many nice things happening out there
> They've never even seen a clue
> But we're doing fine
> Making memorable rhyme
> And know we've doing our part
> I've got a Caribbean soul I can barely control
> And some Texas hidden here in my heart

Crosby, Stills and Nash's "Southern Cross" and "Short on Underwear," a sailing saga they recorded from a tape that was being circulated around the boatyard, were standards. But when everyone was tired of everything, Ivory's collection of jazz standards, show tunes and Latin instrumentals never failed as, hour-by-hour, day-by-day, the progress continued.

In the beginning, Jeffrey deep down inside, was sure his mom and dad were kidding him about the summer. No matter how much they talked to him about working on the boat, Jeffrey could not mentally let go of the notion that somehow, he was going to wiggle out of it and spend this summer like last summer, at the country club, at one with nature and "Big Bertha," and hopefully, Lynn. *They wouldn't do this to him.*

Disbelief turned to anger as he found himself at one with the *Harlequin* and a big "Sioux" slow-speed grinder that weighed at least 15 pounds. At first, he tried to act klutzy and ill-suited for the work thinking he'd wear them down.

"Jeffrey, I'm paying you a good hourly wage. Quit complaining. I guess you could refuse to do the work, but, gosh, Jeff, think about college and all those beautiful girls waiting to introduce themselves to you."

"Dad." *God, I hate him.*

He couldn't understand what they were trying to prove. What in the hell was he going to learn by grinding a piece of metal? How was he going to find 'the zone,' that cosmic time and place on the golf course when it all comes together, while holding a tool named after a Native American tribe? How was he ever going to get Lynn back if he couldn't visit her by the country club pool? *Fucking ass-*

holes.

"You won't be grinding all summer. After you're finished with the seams, you are going to coat everything in Ospho, a rust inhibitor, then you're going to paint the hull with primer before the final coat of paint. Those and many other exciting projects lie in store for you, you lucky boy."

"What about my friends?"

"Jeff, you've got a summer job. You'll survive, other people just like you have in the past and will in the future. If you're not too tired, you can go out in the evenings."

Now that his father and mother had had this mysterious reawakening and his girlfriend had said she wanted "space," Jeff's life was totally miserable.

Yet he had no other options because next year he would be moving away from home, going to college—four expense-paid, unchaperoned years. He couldn't throw his life away for one summer of shit work. Charlie tried to tell him that it wasn't because of the car wreck. He kept saying it had something to do with perspective and learning about life, whatever the fuck that meant. *So stupid, stupid, stupid.*

That afternoon, tears filled Jeff's eyes as he let go of the trigger on the grinder. Picturing himself finishing the 18th hole and walking by the glistening swimming pool where Lynn would be tan and waiting in her bikini, he could visualize her thighs and the outline of her chest. He could smell the manicured grass and feel the cart bumping along the paths next to the fairways, and it was free. All he had to do was sign the ticket—Jeff Jones, #92, 15% gratuity included.

Pulling off his dust mask, he walked towards the water's edge that was about 150 feet from where the *Harlequin's* hull was resting on steel supports. The only thing left of his pathetic love life was a video cassette of *Debbie Does Dallas,* the X-rated video hidden in his closet. God, he hoped she wasn't fucking anyone. It was killing him.

Big help Ivory was. Coming back from having his teeth cleaned, he told Jeff to forget about Lynn and find someone who wants to be a dental hygienist. "Look," Ivory said, "they make good money so there'll always be food on the table. Your teeth will be clean. And the best part is, after a day of talking to people who can't talk back, there is a chance she might want to listen to what you have to say. Think of it, a wife who listens!"

"Real funny, Ivory."

What they're doing to me isn't right. This meaning-of-life shit shouldn't be happening at the <u>most important time in my life.</u>

Hurting, suffering, in the depths of his despair and

parental loathing, in the depths of his profound loneliness, standing hot, dirty and sweaty with the gray Sioux 2000 RPM grinder in his hand, he caught a glimpse of the car as it turned into the marina.

Going too fast, it stopped abruptly on the loose dirt when she saw him. As the dust trailing her car caught up and settled, she pulled down the visor mirror. Shaking her head, she arranged her hair and put her sunglasses back on. Lipstick. Check.

Then ... she swung those legs out of the car.

Smiling, Lynn walked over to Jeff and put her hand on his grimy, sweaty arm, before she looked up at this monster boat that he was working on.

The enormity took her by surprise, causing her mouth to open slightly as she removed her sunglasses. Squinting in the bright, hot sunlight, brow furrowed, eyes darting from one thing to the next, mouth still partially opened, she slowly breathed those sacred words—"Holy fucking cow."

Towering in front of her was a gargantuan, raw steel sailboat hull, a bigger-than-life monolith named the *Harlequin*—an overwhelming iron sculpture that cast a long shadow over them as her keel rested on dry land.

The *Harlequin* was in the Laguna Madre Marine boatyard in the company of two steel working shrimp boats, about 80 feet long and 25 feet wide with towering outriggers, a handful of sailboats in the 40-foot range as well as a few smaller commercial fishing boats.

Lynn, in her white linen shorts and beige blouse, sunglasses in hand, squinted as she walked around the hull. The steel was dark gray and black in places. In others, mostly around the welded seams, there was some terracotta-colored rust.

As they stepped back and looked at her from the bow, she gradually expanded into the roundness of her midsection before retreating to her more narrow stern. As large as a shrimper, she was the size one would imagine the whale that swallowed Jonas might be. Metal braces with pads—three starboard and three port—supported the hull from the sides as the full keel rested on wood blocks.

After circling, Lynn climbed the ladder first. Following her up, Jeff was able to catch a glimpse of her underwear as she stepped over the gunwale and onto the deck where she touched the cabin side with her manicured fingers.

Staring at her standing on the unfinished steel deck, he wanted to softly kiss the small freckle on the back of her neck and then unbutton her blouse right there in the daylight. At that same moment, she felt a frightening attraction to whatever these people were doing with this big *thing* that could sail, like, around the world.

She turned, "Jeff, this is way cool. This is the coolest thing I have ever seen in my entire whole life." Smelling like a working man, he had never looked better.

That night she called, "Tell me everything."

Building a boat that you could live on and sail anywhere in the world—California, Tahiti, Monaco, México—this wasn't boring. This was daring. This had plot. This way she could get to know Evett ... and be around Jeff.

Jeff did learn one thing *fast*—there is nothing sexier than a woman in a baseball cap doing physical labor. Without self-awareness, she would be concentrating on the task at hand—leaning over, climbing over and holding pieces in place. Soon she would be Evett's right-hand woman.

One of the greatest gifts the *Harlequin* gave back to those spending their time, effort, sweat and tears to create, was time to *think*.

This was the answer to Jeff's question about how he could possibly benefit from mindless work. It doesn't occupy the mind. It gives the brain time and freedom to wander. Left alone, it conjures up all sorts of thoughts. Uncluttered, untethered, it can recreate a sexual encounter or pull up odd memories from out of nowhere. It can do whatever the hell it wants, and there's not much a person doing mindless work can do about it.

There may be a "zone" in golf. There definitely is a "zone" in construction.

During a typical day, doing something physical, like sanding, or welding, the arms fatigue rapidly to the point the body may not think it can go on. But just before it gives up, it enters into the "zone" and can go on for hours while the mind entertains itself like an in-flight movie, except the "in-flight" movie is your own mind's full-color creation of your life—past, present, future.

And, the more often the mind is left alone to think, the better it becomes at it. Not only can it pull obscure files from the past, it can create a funny scenario. It can lament unconsummated lust and then create what would have been had the moment been seized. It can digress or go fast forward or simply go over something again and again until it's ready to let go.

Red, watching her torch cut through metal or the bead of steel bonding two pieces together through a welder's hood, could relive the good times and almost feel Hal's touch.

Susan couldn't help but wonder whether what she had done artistically was in any way significant. Why she did what she did, she concluded, was for herself. That's why Ivory played music, even when no one was listening.

Not many paintings end up in the Louvre in Paris, and few Egyptian vases have survived. Her paintings, most probably, would be stored in someone's futuristic garage until they decided to clean house. The odds of her paintings surviving "forever" was nil—nothing lasts forever, nothing stays the same.

Susan thought back to the clown painting she had included in her "Blood on the Cabbage" series and decided that artists are the real clowns—the harlequins—finding ways to get attention.

Ivory, pulling up image after image of his youth, saw himself driving from town to town in his beat-up Model-T. He could distinctly hear Hoover's voice on the radio—the monotone assurances that it was, in effect, better for people to starve than be morally ruined by governmental handouts. He remembered well the euphoria of Roosevelt's election.

Hysterical and scary at the same time, it was impossible to believe the huge controversy Scott Joplin's ragtime had caused. Ivory could vaguely remember evangelist Aimee Semple McPherson voice over the radio. "In Christian homes, where purity and morals are stressed, ragtime should find no resting place. Avaunt ragtime rot!"

The irony of music's evolution was its source. This new music didn't come from the higher academies of music or the symphony halls of Europe, the source for ragtime and jazz was the cotton fields, which you could see in the distance, standing on top of the *Harlequin*.

Swing. The Eastern big bands lapped it up, and so did the cowboys out West. Duke Ellington, Benny Goodman, Glenn Miller were swinging on the East Coast, while Bob Wills and Spade Cooley, wearing cowboy hats, were swinging in the Southwest and West Coast. The fascinating part was they were all drinking from the same trough—the blues. Much of the difference in sound was the difference in instruments and how they were played. Pianos were too heavy for covered wagons. Guitars and fiddles weren't. It wasn't until trains connected the vast continent that pianos became household entertainment centers.

The beer halls, the melodramas, the hobos, the trains, the bands—long-forgotten faces reappeared as Ivory's right hand sanded the port-side teak bookshelf. He remembered well his big break and the contract he signed with RKO Pictures, and naturally, he remembered seeing Evett for the first time on the motion picture lot. Once again, he was able to see her for the first time without her clothes and feel her arms around him as they locked in. None of the others had a clue that old man Ivory was fantasizing about fucking his wife for the first time.

He saw his son and daughter grow up and heard

the songs he played with people who were now old-timers like himself. The big difference in Evett's thoughts were that many of them, especially the early ones, were in Spanish. Her mind went back and forth.

She and Lynn became bosom buddies, yakking endlessly about theater with Ivory chiming in every now and then. For years Evett had been the heart and soul of the Corpus Christi Community Theater, putting on show-after-show, year-after-year. They'd even put on *Hair*.

Evett, deeply into Texas politics, had become friends with Molly Ivins, the *Fort Worth Star-Telegram* columnist, and Ann Richards who was making a name for herself in her quest to be the new governor.

Perhaps the person most affected by self-examination was Charlie and his renewed awareness of what his parents' aspirations and disappointments had been—how they'd maintained their perspective throughout. He'd had a hard time understanding them growing up. Now, Charlie's jaw tightened when he thought about how proud he was of them charting their course as best they could through a maze of circumstances not of their own making.

The added construction bonus: everyone got to learn how to do everything they wanted. Lynn was welding.

Chapter XXIV

The *Harlequin* Gets Wet

FROM a skateboarding metalhead, Jeff had, for the love of a woman, transformed into a Corpus Christi Country Club brat—golf, underage kid slipping the bartender an extra buck for a beer, talking the country club talk.

But, when his parents shot that persona down due to some type of mid-life crisis problem they were apparently having, Jeff had no choice other than to go along no matter how painful it was. There was too much at stake.

Then, when he was about as low as a person could possibly go, Lynn had miraculously come back. Of course, Ivory kidded him about it.

"Jeff, look at yourself through a woman's eyes and

think of Darwin. If you were a woman, wouldn't you be attracted to someone with exceptional grandparents who isn't afraid to work with his hands and get scuffed up? Feel those muscles, boy," Ivory said as he good-naturedly pushed his thumb into Jeff's biceps. "Wouldn't *you* want a woman who wants to put her arms around you instead of some weenie in a pink golf shirt? ... Maybe you could talk her into being a dental hygienist."

Late in the afternoon around sunset, Jeff and Lynn started taking walks to the pier next to Laguna Madre Marine where they would dangle their legs over the side, looking down at the small, silver fish circling the barnacle-encrusted pilings. As the sun went down, birds would start coming to roost in nearby trees as the color of the sky changed from blue to pink.

Sitting on the wood dock, she confessed that the main reason she was angry with him after the car wreck was she'd been worried the scar and the cap on her tooth would hurt her camera persona.

Fearing ridicule, Lynn had kept her desire to be an actress to herself. Now, for the first time she felt comfortable talking to Jeff and working with Evett. The more time they spent together, the more she began to better understand the craft, and that acting isn't a beauty contest.

"Jeff, what are you going to be? What do you want

to do?" she asked, as she opened a beer from the small cooler they'd brought and handed it to him before opening one for herself. Jeff said he didn't know, honestly, he didn't have a clue.

Red's dog, Jim, and Bojangles had become boatyard dogs, sleeping in the shade of the hull, playing in the flats, watching and chasing fish. They always followed Jeff and Lynn to the pier where they'd lie down next to them, tired at the end of a boatyard day.

"I could pick you up after dinner, and we could take a drive back here to rehearse a love scene. I've got the key to the trailer and there's some beer in the cooler."

The next morning at the boatyard, Jeff and Lynn had smiles on their faces as they helped the rest of the crew prop up the section of steel Red had cut out of the hull so they could enter and exit like Noah's zebras and lions. It took all six of them using two hydraulic jacks and three four-by-four timbers to leverage it into place. Once there, Red spot- welded it and then permanently welded it.

The last job Jeff, with Lynn's help, was going to do before school started was fair in the seam around Noah's door—then prime and paint it. This was their shared moment in the spotlight, and they damn sure were going to do it so well the seam couldn't be seen, which took skill and an acquired eye. The rest of the hull was done.

After much back-and-forth with color charts, the final decision was the *Harlequin* should be painted "Nantucket Green" to go along with the white decks and wheelhouse. The color would dress her up some.

"Good work, kid," Charlie said, and put his arm around Jeff's neck and pulled him close. A family can go on a vacation together, they can ski Aspen together, they can visit the pyramids of Egypt together and they will hopefully become closer to each other, but there's nothing like building a boat together. The ups, the downs, the fights, the satisfaction of seeing progress—the closeness.

All that remained by summer's end was deck and detail work that could be done once she was in the water. It was time to dismantle the worksite and do all the last-minute things that needed to be done before she got wet.

No doubt the launch was going to be exciting. At the same time, it was sad to take apart the world that had been theirs for almost two years. It symbolized a new beginning and, at the same time, the end of an experience that was painful, hot, happy, uplifting, gratifying—all those things and more. The shed that housed the tools would remain until it was time to take it back to Harlequin Oil, but the spot of dirt the boat occupied was soon going to be an empty one and the roles people played were going to change.

The travel lift with tires six feet tall lumbered toward the *Harlequin* at a snail's pace. Straddling the roof, the eye bolts Hal had put on the top were hooked and the tin roof was lifted from its supports. Slowly, slowly the lift carried it from over the *Harlequin* and lowered it off to the side.

As the sun illuminated the fresh paint, not many words were spoken over the noise of the diesel engine. Susan put her arm around Charlie, whose eyes moistened just a little as the shed roof dangled from the plodding machine that would soon be lifting the *Harlequin* and lowering her into the water.

Lynn put her arm through Jeff's and gave him a squeeze. Ivory, Evett and Red stood close by.

The weather had cooled by October 22, Hal's birthday, nine days before Halloween. It was only fitting that this should be the launch day.

Sheets of butcher paper protected the painted hull from the foot-wide straps that would lift the hull up from its supports and carry her to the launch slip. From this point, until the boat was in the water, the boatyard crew was in control. They did it every day—pull 'em out and put 'em back in.

No one stood still. Evett and Susan were both taking pictures as they nervously milled around looking at the suspended hull as it moved ever closer to the water. Evett walked over to Lynn for a while as Ivory and Jeff pointed and talked. No one could hear what the others were saying over the noise.

A bottle of Korbel champagne had been wrapped with masking tape to keep it from shattering at the christening. Carrying it by the neck, Red got ready when the *Harlequin,* still suspended, was over the water. As the lift began to lower her, Red hit the "V" of the bow harder than she needed to before she and the others watched a real parting of the seas. Evett caught the exact moment the bottle exploded along with Red's expression on her Nikon camera with Kodachrome.

Once completely in the water, they all jumped on board to check for hull leaks or water coming in through the thru-hulls. Everything was A-okay. The *Harlequin* was floating. On land she had been solid as a rock. But now she was gently moving with the breeze in the saltwater that was her new home.

After the "all clear," Red gave the launch crew a thumbs-up, so they could free the straps and tie her off. No rush. After checking things for a good half hour, Charlie pushed the start button for the main engine—nothing. Then Charlie remembered he had turned off the main battery switch while the battery charged overnight. He went below deck and turned the large lever from "Off" to "Bat 1" and climbed the steps to the wheelhouse companionway.

This time the engine turned over for about 15 seconds before a cylinder caught, then another, a big puff of white smoke blew out of the exhaust as the *Harlequin* began pulsating. She was alive. She had oil pressure.

Charlie immediately went down to the engine room to make sure water was flowing through the filter that cooled the six-cylinder "Jimmy." The green-colored engine was running cool, vibrating slightly as it idled. When Red poked her head through the engine room door to see what he was up to, he said they ought to let it run for a half an hour to make sure there was no air in the fuel lines.

For the initial test run they were going to motor up the mile-long channel to the Intracoastal before turning around. Jeff gave the bow a push as an onlooker threw the stern line to Susan. Red pushed the gearshift forward and the engine almost choked before she gave the throttle a nudge. Charlie would have to adjust the idle.

Ivory, having more boating experience than the rest, was helping Red at the helm. The worst that could happen is the *Harlequin* would have to be towed back to the marina by the work skiff.

Advancing the throttle, it felt as though they were

flying through the water though they were only going four knots. Cautiously, Red throttled back and waited until they reached the widened part of the channel where she turned the helm to the right and then hard to the left to make the turn.

Afterwards, Red experimented by shifting the gears into reverse. Ivory carefully coached her on throttling down before she returned the gearshift to neutral. Commanding the helm of a brand new, 48-foot single-screw boat, takes getting used to. With awkwardness they got her into the slip and tied off. She looked so beautiful.

The wind had a chill to it as they brought chairs on deck and opened the cooler where champagne had been iced. Jeff popped the first cork and began pouring while Charlie popped the second.

Together, they raised their glasses to Captain Red—and the person who had made this *Harlequin* possible—Hal.

Chapter XXV

Port Isabel

RED and Jim slept on board that first night. Her bird dog had become her closest companion, the one she talked to when no one else was around.

Awake at first light, the landscape was a changed one. The piece of earth where the keel had been laid and the *Harlequin* had been built was now vacant. Off to the side was the trailer, wood picnic table and tool shed.

Sitting on deck with Jim at her feet, Red had a long talk with Hal as the *Harlequin* floated peacefully in the water—her first morning afloat.

The night before, she had given Jeff the key to her Robstown house so he and Lynn could be alone together.

In the guest bedroom, they made love, yet the most satisfying part was simply being close to each other and talking in bed afterward. *Something momentous had happened, and they knew it.*

Jeff got home around midnight after dropping Lynn off. Surprised to find his parents still out by the pool. Sitting awfully close to each other, he realized he might have interrupted a real kiss. *Oh man, I'm out of here.* In bed, he wouldn't get to sleep for hours.

Ivory and Evett, propped up on pillows, were going through dozens of pictures they had taken of the crew as they were building the *Harlequin*. They'd seen and done a lot in their lifetime, but nothing like this. What a grand accomplishment and how great it was to work with their very own son, Charlie, Susan and the kids.

The next day, Susan and Charlie arrived in the early afternoon. He was anxious to go below to the engine room and fire up each generator individually. Because the air conditioners were water-cooled, they were the next to be run for the first time. There was so much to do.

"Susan, it was the least tortured sleep I have had in I don't know how long—once I finally got to sleep. The stars were out and the moon came up so clearly. I could hear the water against the hull. How will I ever be able to repay you for what you've done for me?"

"Don't worry, you will. You're going to be so sick of having us hanging around, you'll regret knowing us, believe me," Susan said as she put her arm around Red's shoulders, "Don't get mushy on me now, girl, we have come too far, and we still have a long way to go."

The whole interior needed another coat of varnish. The bulkheads that were painted "Marfil," an eggshell white enamel, needed a final coat. The propane stove wasn't hooked up. Charlie wasn't through with the refrigeration system. The decks needed a final coat of Awlgrip with non-skid mixed in. On deck, the 50-foot aluminum mast had to be stepped and rigged. The awning frame had to be constructed so Evett and Lynn could sew the awning to size, etc.

Hal had designed the wheelhouse and the forward deck to be as open as possible because that is where he felt the most time would be spent. Below deck was light and airy, but the point of having a boat was to enjoy the outdoors—seeing the pelicans and the sea gulls, seeing the sun rise and set.

The *Harlequin's* primary source of power was its "GM Jimmy" Detroit 6-71 diesel. In addition to the main engine there were two Onan diesel generators.

If the engine failed, the sails were more than steadying sails. In theory, 10 knots of wind could power the boat a respectable 50 or 60 degrees to weather, meaning that by tacking she could make progress even against the wind. All of this would have to be tried out, but Charlie and Ivory had a hunch that, if anything, the performance would be better than Hal's estimates because he tended to guess on the conservative side.

Charlie, based on Hal's plans, had put together a compact, functional engine room that was clean and white, except for the green Detroit Diesel in the center. There wasn't a knuckle-buster anywhere. Engine alignment, bilge, everything was right there. The *Harlequin* was self-contained. She carried 800 gallons of water, 500 gallons of diesel fuel, propane for cooking, batteries for 12-volt power and generators for 110-volt electricity.

Lynn's parents were trying hard to keep up with their daughter who had suddenly become talkative—about things they didn't understand. It was going to be an incredible maiden voyage, she gushed. On Friday nights and at school she was still the blond, bombshell cheerleader yelling through her monogrammed megaphone. Away from school, running around with Jeff at the boatyard, she could come home so filthy she needed a brush to get the dirt from underneath her fingernails.

If this wasn't unnerving and confusing enough to keep them on edge, Lynn was unusually, naturally sexual—everything about her was provocative. Just looking at her was to confront temptation because you want to see all of her. A blond version of a younger Evett, she couldn't tie her shoelaces without people gawking.

How could her parents not let their split-personality, over-sexed paradoxical daughter go on the maiden voyage? "Bon voyage."

The initial sail would be to Port Isabel, 120 nautical miles to the southwest, on this side of the Río Grande from Matamoros, México. It would be a safe test because the Intracoastal Waterway is protected from the Gulf of México by Padre Island, a long barrier island.

Two days after Christmas, they uncleated the lines, coiled and stored them in the locker aft of the wheelhouse.

Lynn's dad in a blue Izod shirt, her mother in a white starched blouse wearing gold earrings, waved goodbye to Lynn and the others from the shore. Red powered forward, toward the narrow channel that led from Laguna Madre Marine to the Intracoastal Waterway. Although a norther was in the forecast, they departed on a beautifully clear winter morning with the temperature in the mid-seventies. The day's destination was Baffin Bay, only 20 miles from Laguna Madre Marine.

Once in the channel, Red turned the bow into the wind as Charlie, Jeff and Lynn unfurled the mainsail. Fifteen knots with gusts up to 20 was going to be a perfect amount of wind to test her sailing power.

As the breeze filled the sail, the *Harlequin* heeled over slightly and then heeled over slightly more as the genoa was set. Ivory helped Susan wench in the foresail. Once the course was set, Red shut down the engine, leaving only the sounds of the gods. Without diesel power, their speed was between six and seven knots—more than enough to get where they were going.

Oh my goodness, these were thrilling moments with a lot of activity on deck.

By noon, Jeff was down to a T-shirt and Lynn was down to her swimsuit top and cut-offs as she and Jeff sat on cushions forward of the awning, talking. Every now and then, they'd hang out over the bow to look at the hull cutting through the water. Mesmerized, they felt like dolphins as the *Harlequin* rose and fell with the sea. Steering was a novelty, especially under sail, so they all took turns at the helm. On their right, to starboard, was mainland Texas and on their left, to port, were Padre Island's glistening white sand dunes. Expecting the norther to hit sometime that night, they snuggled in as close as they could to the south side of a small island in Baffin Bay and dropped the storm hook.

Ivory knew several good fishing spots up close to

the shoreline of the King Ranch, so he, Charlie, Lynn and Jeff got into the new skiff and off they went. Lynn was the most excited. She had never caught a fish before.

Evett, Susan and Red, stayed onboard the *Harlequin* stretching out on the cushions they'd made to fit the cabin top. It was such a gloriously carefree feeling to be out in the wild on a perfect day—watching the seagulls and lazy clouds as they floated above—from *the HARLEQUIN*!

Skimming across the water in the Boston Whaler, Charlie couldn't help but remember the days back when he, his dad and some amigos with boats like their wooden 14-footer, would go down the Intracoastal for an overnight campout. They'd pitch tents in the dunes and the kids would play "flashlight" in the dark. The boats were so small and the outboards so unreliable, they made the trip in a group in case one had trouble.

The *Harlequin's* "tender" was stable and unsinkable with a dependable 25 horsepower Johnson.

Using live shrimp rigged to a popping cork, Lynn reeled in maybe 10 speckled trout that were keepers. Big excitement—netting the fish, the slimy blood on the deck, pulling the hook out its mouth and putting the fish on ice.

To go along with the fried fish, Ivory and Evett had brought their special tartar sauce and salsa picante. No food had ever tasted better. The entire crew was tired by the time they'd cleaned up after dinner.

Sitting on deck, savoring the day and how the *Harlequin* had performed, everyone bundled up as the temperature dropped. With the stars and moon blanketing them in the clear, cool air, all was well, except with Red who missed her husband, her lover, *her* boatbuilder, very, very much.

Just after two in the morning, as expected, the breeze freshened. Charlie was the first to hear the north wind whistling through the rigging so he went down below, brushed his teeth using the freshwater hand pump and climbed the teak companionway steps back up to the wheelhouse.

Everyone got up for a while, until the monotony of staring into the darkness and watching rain hit the windows set in.

The norther's leading edge with gusting winds passed through quickly leaving only an overcast sky with a slight drizzle for Charlie who stayed on watch while everyone else went back to their bunks. The warmth and smell of the mesquite fire that Jeff had built in the ship's fireplace found its way up to the wheelhouse as Charlie sat in the swiveling helmsman's chair. With a blanket covering Susan, she fell asleep in the berth beside him.

Before settling in for the night watch and turning off the spreader lights leaving only the anchor light, Charlie got up again to walk the side decks, check the anchor chain and pull on the rigging as he looked up the mast at the furled sails. Before going inside, he leaned over once more to look at her sides and marvel at how magnificent she was.

Opening and quickly closing the wheelhouse door behind him, Charlie took off his foul weather jacket and, after rubbing his hands together, went down the companionway to the galley, which was on the starboard side. Warm and cozy inside, it was dark and cold outside.

Charlie took his time pouring a couple of fingers of dark rum into a porcelain cup from the shelf. With Red spending the nights between the *Harlequin* and the house in Robstown, the ship looked comfortably lived in. The galley had spices.

A faint light from the fire in the soapstone and bronze fireplace shimmered off the varnished bookshelves on port and starboard sides above the settees, the shadows radiating a presence that was eerily ghostlike. On the port side was the grand table with varnished teak leaves and fiddles.

Forward of the main saloon, was Red's stateroom. Further forward were two more double staterooms. All the doors were varnished, louvered teak except for the head doors, which were white-paneled with teak frames. The cabin sole was solid teak.

At eye level there were six bronze opening ports on each side.

Cup in hand, Charlie climbed back up to the wheelhouse where, outside, the only visible object was a flashing green channel marker Charlie was using as a reference point to make sure the anchor was holding.

We did it. We actually did it. We pulled it off ... kept ricocheting around in his mind. *We took the moment and grabbed it.*

Staring out into the darkness.... At least no one's calling me serious Charlie anymore. *Fucking "A" I was serious ... my dark skin, moreno, came from pigment. Since the last thing I wanted to do was work in a hardware store, I knew I was on my own. Mom was a fucking movie star and she still had difficulty navigating Texas. I knew from the get-go that nobody but me was going to take care of this Mexican boy.*

He smiled to himself—that's our house on Ocean Drive. I'm the one the Armani "suits" from New York City say, "Yes, sir," to.

Now the *Harlequin's* got us all up messed up. We are not who we were. We'll never be the same.

Jeff, and Lynn, they're for sure in trouble. After building a boat there isn't much that seems undoable. They know hardware stores—*Jones Hardware was the best*—and how to cuss with conviction. They can joke around with fishermen and josh with the guys behind the counter. They're not embarrassed to ask questions and know how to work with their hands. Next year they're going to be with college kids that don't know shit from Shinola. How's that going to play out? Maybe the best thing we learned in our own subconscious way was that when something fucks up, let it go, and start figuring out what you've got to do going forward to get the job done.

And you, Hal, dammit to hell we did it, didn't we, all of us? ... me? There are things Susan and I need to do. It's up to each of us to fill the "unforgiving minute." In 50 years no one will even know I existed, and why should they?

Dawn greeted them with a light rain and a cold, gray sky. Inside the wheelhouse it was warm and cozy as Red and Susan watched Charlie, Jeff and Lynn, in yellow foul-weather gear, work the windlass and raise the 80-pound anchor. To get the mud off the flukes, they had to lower and raise it several times.

Secured, Red put the "Jimmy" in gear and headed for the channel. Off to port they could see the waves breaking offshore on the other side of the dunes. The much smaller white caps on Baffin Bay were nothing for the *Harlequin's* 40 feet of waterline slicing through the waterway. Profound. A tinge scary when they thought about it.

Charlie now at the helm, looked over at Susan who was motionlessly staring out of the rain-spotted windows—the softness of her hair, the curves of her neck, her talent, her mind and the incredible fact that they were together. *Now look what they had gone and done.*

From out of nowhere came the vague memory of his high school trip to Nuevo Laredo and the soft-bellied whore.

Port Isabel ... Isabel, Isabel ... It came to him. That was her name, the bleached blond girl at "La Luz Roja." It was Isabel who had played her part in getting Charlie to Sunday school where Susan came to his rescue. Without Isabel would they have blushingly rendezvoused in Susan's lacy bedroom? They were so young—16?

In the distance, on the flat Texas horizon, he could see a water tower and the outline of buildings where the *Harlequin* and crew should arrive well before dark.

THE END

OTHER WORKS by BEN HARRISON

Books
Undying Love
Sailing Down the Mountain
The Rooster Who Loved the Violin
Official Visit

Music Albums
Duval Years
Erin Elkins and Ben Harrison
Side Effects
Destino
Air Sunshine
El Isleño 1921

Musicals
Key West: A Musical Tour About Town
Undying Love - The Musical
Clouds Over the Sunshine Inn
El Isleño 1921: The Untold Key West Story

ACKNOWLEDGEMENTS

I would like to thank Helen Harrison and Chloe Bygren, for doggedly and repeatedly proofreading CHARLIE JONES, my one-and-only novel. Artist, Melinda K. Hall, my sister Julie Harrison Holland and Jane Lee Lade also gave it a run-through. "Y'all," they know the challenge of editing a mixture of Texan and grammar.   - BH

Made in the USA
Monee, IL
10 November 2025

34192409R00171